Because We Can!

a Donovan Creed Novel - Volume 11

John Locke

D0542309

TELEMACHUS PRESS

This book is a work of fiction. Names, characters, places and incidents are either the product of the author's imagination or are used fictitiously. Any resemblance to actual persons, living or dead, or to actual events or locales is entirely coincidental.

BECAUSE WE CAN!

Cover Designed by: Telemachus Press, LLC
Copyright © Shutterstock/ 140496517

Published by: Telemachus Press, LLC at Smashwords
http://www.smashwords.com
http://www.telemachuspress.com

Visit the author website:
http://www.donovancreed.com

ISBN: 978-1-939927-52-1 (eBook)
ISBN: 978-1-939927-53-8 (Paperback)

Printed in the United States of America

10 9 8 7 6 5 4 3 2 1

For Erin Roche-Wise and John E. Roche.
Entertaining you has been an honor and a privilege.

Because We Can!

PART ONE:
How Maybe Taylor Got Involved

Chapter 1

Jake and Lemon.

"WHAT? BULLSHIT!"

"I swear to God."

"You fucked Lemon Fister?"

"Jesus, Brody. Keep your voice down."

"Fine. I'll whisper it. You seriously mean to sit there and tell me that you, Jake Stallone, fucked Lemon Fister."

"That's right."

"*Our* Lemon Fister?"

"You know any others?

They're at Harry's Nickel, trendy bar, corner booth. A young waitress with frosted hair approaches. "Hi guys, I'm Alice."

"Wow!" Brody says. "Just so you know, I'm available."

Jake says, "That's something she doesn't hear often enough."

Alice smiles, bends at the waist, props her elbows on the table so they can check out her implants.

Jake knows a practiced move when he sees one. "Who taught you tip-whoring, your mom?"

"*Jesus, Jake!*" Brody says. "I'm sorry, Alice. My friend's a jerk. I'm Brody, by the way."

She winks at him. "All part of the job. So, you guys ready to order?"

They do, and Brody watches her ass as she snakes through the crowd. Then turns to Jake and says, "That was rude, even for you."

"Yeah, it was. I hate prick-teasers."

"She's not like that."

"Oh, really?" Jake laughs. "If she so much as remembers your name, I'll apologize."

"You're on! So. Where were we?"

"Lemon Fister."

"Right. Swear it. On your life."

"I swear on my life."

"You lying motherfucker!"

Jake smiles. "It's true. My crowning achievement."

"It's insane! How the fuck did—wait. Does Faith know?"

"Of course not."

Brody shakes his head. "You son of a bitch! Okay, so who else knows?"

"No one."

"*What?* I can't be trusted with this information!"

"Sorry, dude. You're my best friend. If I can't trust you, who can I trust?"

"I need details."

"Like what?"

"Like everything. I mean, how long has this been going on?"

"Six months."

"Six *months?* And you're just *now* telling me? Why now?"

"I couldn't hold it in any longer."

"What, this bombshell revelation? Or your dick?"

"Both."

"She's—wait. How old is she?"

"Thirty-two. Today."

Brody sighs. "I am so fucking jealous. I hate you. You know that, right?"

"Your envy's a huge part of the fun. Why else would I tell you?"

"Because you're an asshole?"

Jake smiles.

Brody thinks a minute. Then says, "Lemon's birthday dinner."

"What about it?"

"Are you *kidding?* I can't *wait* to see the two of you in the same room!"

"I may not go."

"*What?* You *have* to go! We're *all* going."

"I might show up late."

"Jake. Look at me. It's a *surprise* party. You need to get there *before* Lemon shows up."

Alice arrives with the drinks.

Brody grins. "I love you, Alice."

She grins back. "I love you, too, Benny."

Jake laughs.

Brody's face falls. "It's Brody."

Alice says, "Aw, shit. I'm sorry."

When she turns he doesn't bother checking her ass. Instead, he looks at Jake and says, "You're fucking Lemon."

"I am."

"You lucky bastard."

"I know. She's amazing."

"Where'd you do it that first time?"

"At a hotel, during her lunch break."

Brody closes his eyes, tries to conjure it in his mind.

He sighs. "You lucky bastard!"

"So you said."

Chapter 2

Milo and Faith.

MILO NEVER KILLED anyone before.

Nor has he killed anything bigger than a bug in his entire life. As for guns, he's done exactly ten minutes at a rifle range. Twenty years ago, as a teenager.

But for this job, experience won't be a factor.

He tries the back door, finds it unlocked, enters the hall.

Milo's been here a dozen times, knows the layout. If you're facing the house, he's at the far right. Master bedroom's far left.

He studies the hallway photos. Faith with her parents. Jake with his arm around her. Faith in her wedding dress, Jake in his tux. The whole gang grinning like fools on the ski slope two years ago, three-quarters drunk.

5

Better days, those.

He moves quietly through the kitchen, then the den, then the foyer. Now, in the far hall, he sees the master bedroom door closed. He puts his ear to it, hears nothing. Slowly turns the handle, pushes the door open a crack. Waits.

Pushes it open some more.

Stands there, waiting for...

For what?

Milo knows where she is. He can hear her in the shower. What he's thinking, he'd love to see Faith Stallone naked. He's seen her in a bikini, of course. All the wives wear them on the beach trips. They're all in great shape. Gracie and Wren are cosmetically enhanced, but the others have managed to maintain the gifts they were born with. Years of Pilates, yoga, and aerobics have rendered them fat-resistant. At thirty-eight, Faith has a few years on Lemon and Lexi, and though Lemon's the clear stunner of the group, Faith is barely a half-step behind.

Especially her face.

Specifically, her mouth.

Milo appreciates Faith's body as much as the next man, but what he loves most is her mouth. There's something bewitching about it. He's only seen one movie star with that mouth, and it's a tough comparison, because of the age difference.

Juno Temple.

Look it up.

Not the smiley version, the pouty one.

6

Faith has Juno Temple's mouth, and Milo's had more than one fantasy about it.

But he'd rather see her naked.

And to do that, he has to enter the bedroom.

He pushes the door open, slips inside, closes it behind him. Master suite is set up bedroom first, then hallway, then master bath. Left side of hallway is Jake's walk-in closet, right side is Faith's.

From where he's standing, Milo can see the entrance to the master bath, and the giant marble tub at the far end. He can see part of the vanities on either wall, but not the toilet on the left or shower on the right.

If Faith was taking a bath, he could see everything.

Of course, that would mean she could see him, too.

And he'd prefer she didn't scream.

Chapter 3

MILO ROUNDS THE bed, opens the top drawer of the end unit, removes Jake's .357.

His first surprise of the evening: the weight of the gun.

He nearly drops it!

He checks to see if it's loaded.

It is.

He carries it to Faith's closet, which he's never seen till this moment.

His second surprise of the evening: the size of her closet. It's huge!

She has four racks of clothes on the left wall. On the right are shelves for shoes, boots, and handbags, and a full-length mirror. There's also a coat closet with louvered slats, and a dressing area in the center of the room.

He figures she'll exit the shower, towel herself dry, enter the closet completely nude. If he hides in her coat closet, he'll get the full monty.

He opens it, pushes some coats out of the way, steps inside, closes the louvered door, and waits.

Thirty seconds pass before she turns off the shower. Twenty more pass quietly while she does whatever she's doing in the bathroom. Then...she enters the dressing area wrapped in an enormous towel that completely covers her body.

Who the hell makes towels that big? Milo wants to know, while silently cursing his bad luck. Still, there's something intoxicating about being a voyeur.

Faith has a hand towel in one hand, cell phone in the other. She glances at herself in the mirror, then presses a button on her phone, and stands it on its side on the shoe shelf.

Surprise number three: she's put the phone on speaker.

"Hello?" Jake says.

"Where are you?"

"Harry's Nickel. Where are you?"

"Home. Just got out of the shower."

She uses the hand towel to dry her hair.

Jake says, "You going someplace?"

"Don't tell me you forgot."

"Remind me."

"Lemon's birthday party? The big event?"

"Oh. Right. I thought you said I could skip it."

"The whole gang's going."

"Guys too? I distinctly remember hearing you say—"

"I did say that. Before I learned the husbands were invited."

They're quiet a minute. Faith says, "It's okay. I'll make up an excuse."

Jake says, "I'll swing by later on. It's at Veluzzi's, right?"

"Right. She'll like that. They all will."

"And you?"

"Of course. But Jake?"

"Yeah?"

"It's a surprise party."

"So?"

"Lemon will be there at seven. If you can't be early, come after seven-fifteen."

"I won't get there before eight."

"Of course you won't. Want me to order for you?"

"Nah. I'll get something here."

"At Harry's?"

"It's happy hour. I'll grab a snack, go home, take a shower. Probably show up at Veluzzi's around eight-thirty. I'll drink while you guys finish your dinner."

"Sounds like you already started drinking."

"You know me. One bourbon. That's my limit."

"One at a time, you mean."

He laughs. "See you later, gator."

"Be safe."

She hangs up, tosses the hand towel on the floor, and—

—Milo nearly gasps as she—

—unwraps the giant towel, stands in the center of the dressing area completely nude, hands on hips, staring at herself in the full-length mirror.

She's...amazing!

Faith turns, Milo gets full-frontal.

Surprise number four: bush. Close-trimmed, but full. You don't see that very often. At least not on the porn sites he frequents.

She turns back to the mirror, cups her breasts, lifts them, frowns. There's no reason for the frown. He'd peg her a 34-C. And firmer than he expected.

As she moves around, he tries to get a better view through the louvered slats....

And bumps the door with the gun.

Faith looks up, eyes wide with shock.

Milo pushes the door open.

Faith gasps. Her eyes go from Milo's face to the gun. She screams, then charges him, catching him off guard.

"You *son of a bitch!*" she yells.

She slaps him once, twice, three times, full force. Then grabs the towel and wraps it around herself. "What the fuck are you *doing* here? You weren't supposed to come till *after* I leave!"

"I wanted to get here early. Make sure I was ready. I didn't know you'd still be here."

"You fucking *pervert!*"

"Look," he says. "Lighten up. I'm killing your husband for you, aren't I?"

"*Are* you? Because from here it looks like you're a degenerate peeping Tom."

"I was concentrating on getting the gun. When I realized you were in the shower I was afraid I'd scare you."

"Oh really? You didn't see the bedroom door was shut? Didn't hear the water running before you came in the bedroom?"

"You've got a gorgeous body. I'm sorry I peeked. I've never done anything like this before."

"Like what, spied on a woman?"

"Killed a man. I'm not thinking straight. It's harder than you think."

She stares him down. Then says. "Forget it. It's a shitty thing to do to me, but I can't forget you're doing me a major favor. Let's move forward. And Milo?"

"Yes?"

"Try to forget what you saw, okay? Because you're never going to see it again."

"Okay."

"Now get out of here while I get dressed."

Chapter 4

"YOU LOOK INCREDIBLE," Milo says, when she enters the bedroom.

"Try not to look at me like that."

"Like what?"

"Like you've seen me naked. It gives me the creeps."

"I'm really sorry about that."

"I'll get over it. I hope. Eventually. *If* you stop staring at me like you've got some sort of secret knowledge. People pick up on that shit."

"I'll be cool."

She studies him a moment. "You don't look so good. You sure you're up for this?"

"I'll get it done."

"Let's hope so."

"You're positive he'll come home before going to the party?"

"One thing about Jake: he's a creature of habit."

"What time do you think he'll get here?"

"Six-thirty, seven at the latest. He'll come in the kitchen, eat some chips and dip. Then he'll come back here, use the bathroom, take a shower. He'll take his time. You heard him on the phone. He intends to show up late for Lemon's party. You know Jake: he'll want to make the grand entrance."

"Too cool to be on time?"

"Exactly. Speaking of which, you're still planning to come, right? After shooting him?"

"Of course."

"Good. Anything else I need to know?"

"Make sure your cell phone's on. Make several calls to different friends while driving to the restaurant. But especially call Jake."

"Why?"

"It'll establish what time you left the house, and prove you went to the party before Jake left Harry's Bar."

"Harry's Nickel."

"Whatever."

"How will it prove that?"

"When the police investigate the shooting you'll be the prime suspect. They'll check your cell phone records, see who you called, and chart your course by the cell towers that picked up your signals."

"You sound like a cop."

Milo shrugs.

Faith says, "Any chance they'll figure it out?"

"I doubt it. You have a bunch of witnesses who'll testify you were at the party. And everyone knows I've been at my mom's house all afternoon. My car's there, and my cell phone. You'll call me at seven-thirty, my mom will answer. You'll talk to her a few minutes, and she'll promptly forget all about it because Alzheimer's a bitch. I'll kill Jake, ride my bike to mom's, grab my phone and car keys, drive to the party. If the police try to check out my alibi they'll get nothing from mom. When they check *your* phone they'll see you called me at seven-thirty, and you'll verify we had a conversation, and you reminded me of the time."

"Don't get caught."

"I won't."

"The reason most people get caught is they trust the wrong person to do the killing. In your case they'll check to see if you're having an affair. You're not, right?"

"We've been through this. I've never been unfaithful."

"And you haven't met anyone you're interested in."

"Not yet."

"And you're not paying me, so there's no transfer of cash from your accounts."

"Right."

"And you haven't bought any insurance on Jake in the past five years?"

"Nope."

"And you haven't been fighting?"

"Nope."

"He's never hit you?"

"No."

"Never cheated on you?"

"Not that I know of."

"So there's no motive for you to kill him, and no motive for me to kill him."

"Correct."

Milo pauses. "Tell me again why you want him dead?"

"I'm sick of him. He disgusts me. And he's cheating on me."

"Cheating? But you just said—"

"I said not that I know of. Meaning, I have no proof. But a wife always knows."

Milo gives her a look. "Are you sure about that?"

"No. But I know he's cheating."

"How?"

"He's way too full of himself lately."

Milo wonders how she can tell. As far as he's concerned, Jake's been full of himself from day one. It's one of the reasons Milo volunteered to kill him. At the time, she thought he was joking. She was upset. He asked if there was anything he could do to cheer her up. "Yeah," she said. "Kill my husband." He said, "I'd love to." She laughed, he didn't. She said, "You could never kill a man." He said, "You might be surprised. All my life I've wondered what it would feel like to take a person's life. I never acted on it because I was afraid I'd get caught. Not to creep you out, but I would definitely do it. For you." She said, "Okay, you're officially scaring me now."

But the following week she brought the subject up again. He couldn't do it on his own, he said, but if the two of them were in on it together, he'd have the confidence to make it happen. He didn't mention he had a huge crush on her, or that he hoped to leverage the murder into a sexual relationship. "Just say the word," he said, and never thought she would.

But here they stand.

Faith says, "Are you going to make it look like a robbery? Because there are things I don't want you to take."

"No. People get in trouble when they try to stage a crime. I'm just going to shoot him, wipe the gun clean, put it back in the drawer, and leave."

"It'll look like a hit."

"I doubt a hit man would use the victim's gun to kill him. But in any case, if there's no motive, and no evidence, it'll be hard for the police to build a case against either of us. Just stay strong, freak out when they tell you he's dead, and don't say anything that could implicate you."

"Like what?"

"Like, 'I can't believe someone shot him!'"

"What's wrong with that?"

"Nothing, if they tell you he was shot. But they probably won't. So try to pretend you know nothing about it."

"What if they ask me to come to the station?"

"Tell them to set it up with your attorney. And Faith?"

She looks at him.

"You can shout, 'Oh my God!' or scream the word, 'No!' several times, or say those things quietly, while crying, but add nothing else, and don't overdo it. Because if you say things like, 'That's impossible!' They'll ask you why it's impossible. If you say, "But I just *heard* from him!" They'll ask you what time, and what you talked about. They'll try to engage you in conversation, but don't fall into their trap."

"What should I say?"

"Stare at them blankly, as if in shock and say nothing. Their best shot at tripping you up is the moment they tell you he's dead. They'll study your reaction and pepper you with questions that seem harmless, but can hang you later."

"I can't just tell them to talk to my attorney the minute they tell me Jake's dead."

"No. But you're well within your rights to be in shock. If you're in shock, it makes sense you can't be responsive. If you feel stuck or cornered, simply pretend to faint. But don't answer any questions. Offer no details. Confirm nothing."

"Won't that make them suspicious?"

"Who gives a shit?"

"Good point."

"Okay," Milo says. "You better get moving."

"Apologize."

"Excuse me?"

"Apologize."

"For what?"

"Spying on me."

"Oh. Look, I'm really sorry about that, Faith. I hope you can forgive me."

"I'll try."

She turns to leave.

Milo says, "Don't forget to call my cell at seven-thirty."

"I'm not an idiot, Milo."

"Sorry. You know me. I'm anal."

He follows her to the garage, waits a few minutes to make sure she's gone, then heads to her closet and goes through her underwear drawer.

Chapter 5

IT STARTED WITH the wives.

Faith, Gracie, and Wren were high school friends turning thirty. Lemon and Lexi were recently married workout buddies, twenty-four. The three met the two at yoga, and became close as sisters within months. The shopping dates, luncheons, and golf outings turned into birthday celebrations and vacations, and by then the husbands were involved. It was one of those rare situations where everyone got along, and it continued, because when you've got a group of ten, and two of the couples have kids, there's always an excuse to get together.

It takes Milo twenty minutes to go through Faith's dresser drawers and bathroom cabinets, and another ten minutes to look through her prescriptions and feminine products. He makes a mental note of her perfume, makeup, and hair products. Not because he anticipates purchasing these items for her in the future, but because...well, just because.

He's not a pervert.

At least, not the way she implied. In other words, sure, he'll stare at a beautiful naked woman if he gets the chance, but he has no interest in trying on her bra and panties, or anything like that.

Except that it's on his mind now, the disgusting things perverts do. Milo wonders what type of satisfaction they could possibly derive by wearing women's underwear.

He'd look it up on the Internet if he had the time, or had a computer handy. He could use his phone, of course, if he'd brought it, but it's a pain trying to find and read things on such a small screen. How much easier to just try on the panties and bra and see if he can figure out what all the fuss is about.

Does he have time?

He puts the gun on the floor of Faith's coat closet, where he hid earlier, and works the killing out in his mind. The best plan is to shoot Jake while he's in the shower. There's a good chance Jake will have his eyes closed or be facing away, which will make the shooting easier. Also, the shower walls and running water will help contain the blood spatter, which should prevent a number of potential crime scene problems.

Of course, when he pulls the shower door open there'll only be three walls to contain the spatter, and Milo will be standing a few feet away. Since he can't afford to let an errant droplet of Jake's blood land on his coat or collar, he decides it makes perfect sense to be completely nude when he shoots his friend.

Milo removes his clothes and checks himself out in Faith's mirror. Then remembers watching her doing the same thing a half hour ago.

After shooing him out of the room she would have put on a bra and panties. When he sees her later tonight, at Lemon's party, she'll be wearing the bra and panties she put on moments after he saw her naked.

He goes back to her underwear drawer, decides on a black, lacy pair of panties, and steps into them. Since Faith is barely half his size, the fit is far from ideal.

But they feel amazing on his skin.

Okay, so silk panties feel great when they belong to your friend's hot wife, the one you've always had a crush on, the one you saw completely naked moments ago. Fine, Milo can accept that.

Doesn't make him a pervert.

Putting on her bra would definitely make him a pervert.

And he's not one.

But again, he wonders why perverts do those sorts of things, and it's not like he's got anything else to do while waiting to shoot Faith's husband.

Two minutes later he's checking himself out in Faith's bra and panties. He thought he'd bust out laughing, but surprise number five, he doesn't look half as silly as he expected. He couldn't possibly fit into her high heels, right?

Right. His feet are way too big.

But what about her platform sandals?

Milo finds a pair with an open heel. He sits on the floor and stuffs his toes in as far as they'll go. He can't buckle the ankle straps, of course, but he ought to be athletic enough to stand and walk. He notes that his heels extend two inches over the back and his toes don't go all the way in, and they're high heels after all, so he'll have to be careful. He gets to his feet, turns to look at himself in the mirror, and crashes to the floor just in time to hear the beep.

Beep?

What beep?

The one that sounds when the back door opens. He heard it when he came in, and heard it again when Faith left.

But why is it beeping now?

Milo wasn't expecting it. Well, obviously he knew it would beep eventually. But he didn't expect to hear it until *after* hearing the garage door open. That's how it's supposed to work, right? Jake comes down the driveway, presses the remote, the garage door slowly opens. Jake waits for it to go up, then drives into the garage, parks his car, presses the re-mote to *close* the garage door, *then* enters the house.

How could Milo not have heard the garage door open?

Because the garage is on the opposite end of the house, you idiot!

He tries to scramble to his feet, but trips and falls again.

Not a problem. Jake's a creature of habit, right? He'll be in the kitchen, eating chips and dip.

Except that Jake turns out to be less a creature of habit than Faith thought. Milo realizes this when he hears Jake barreling down the hallway at a fast clip. Milo crawls on his hands and knees to Faith's coat closet, starts to close the louvered door, and realizes he's left his clothes in a pile in front of her dresser! He dives for them at the precise moment Jake enters the bedroom where Milo waited for Faith while she got dressed. There's no way Milo can get back in Faith's coat closet in time to avoid Jake. He's lying facedown on the floor in the center of Faith's closet, wearing her bra and panties and platform sandals and nothing else.

What to do?

Nothing. There's no solution.

Milo grabs his clothes, covers his head, and...

...By some miracle Jake walks right past him and enters the master bathroom.

Milo scoops up his clothes, makes his way back to the coat closet, closes the door. He quietly removes Faith's sandals, but leaves the bra and panties on.

Then waits to hear the shower running.

Except that what he hears is the TV.

Who watches TV while taking a shower?

No one.

And Jake isn't watching it either. He's listening to it while taking a piss, Milo figures, when he hears the toilet flush. Jake turns the TV volume higher. Milo can't make out the words, but it sounds like a female newscaster. Suddenly Jake shouts, "Twenty-two! Twenty-two! Twenty-two!"

What the hell?

And a moment later, "*Oh my God!* Seventeen! Say it! Say seventeen!"

Jake is shouting. Milo wonders what the fuck's going on. Suddenly Jake shrieks like an impaled banshee. *"No fuckin' way!"* he screams. "No fuckin' WAY!"

He runs down the hall, then back to the bathroom, shouting, "Omigod! Phone! Phone! Where's my fuckin' phone?"

Does Faith want Jake dead because he's crazy? Milo hears the TV go quiet.

Jake shouts, "Answer it!"

Apparently he's found the phone and placed a call. The phone's not on speaker, but Milo hears every word Jake says, because he's pacing up and down the hall between the master bath and bedroom. Every few seconds he spots Jake through the louvered door facing a different direction.

What he realizes, eventually, is Jake, or Faith—or both of them—have just won the lottery.

Chapter 6

"IT DEPENDS ON how many winners there are," Jake says on the phone. "If it's just us, it's $165 million! No, I'm not shitting you!"

He pauses a moment, then says, "I swear on my life!"

Pause. "Cash option? I think they said $107 million and change. No, how many times must I say it? I'm not shitting you! You gotta come celebrate!"

Pause. "*Forget* the fuckin' party!"

Pause. "No, I'm sorry. Of course you need to be there. But what I'm saying, come see me *before* the party. We need to celebrate."

"Yes, of *course* I expect sex! This is the best night of our lives!"

Pause. "I know you're heading there right now. But look. A quickie. Ten minutes. Make it five. How about five? Five minutes. I mean, seriously, I know we've had some issues lately, but this changes everything, don't you see? It changes *everything*! We've got to celebrate. We *need* to celebrate!"

Pause. "Yes, I already told you I'm coming to the party. How can I not? Can you imagine their faces when they hear the news?"

He laughs, then says, "I'll take a shower right now. See you in a few, okay?" Pause. "Thank you! You're the best!"

He dances past the doorway into the master bath, and turns on the shower, leaving Milo thoroughly confused about what to do.

The sonovabitch won the fucking *lottery*? Surely not. And yet, how could anyone be that excited unless they knew for certain?

Jake's in the shower. This is the perfect time to kill him.

Except that Jake was obviously talking to Faith just now, which means she's on her way back home, which means he can't kill Jake without ruining Faith's alibi.

Not to mention if Jake and Faith have truly just won the lottery, killing Jake would give Faith a huge motive for the killing.

It's a crazy situation.

Faith's on her way home, where she knows Milo's waiting to kill her husband. She can't call to tell him *not* to kill Jake, because Milo's phone's at his mom's house.

It's also an *interesting* situation, because Faith knows Milo's hiding in her closet. She'll have to make love to Jake knowing Milo will probably sneak out and peek at them. Sure, she'll insist on doing it somewhere else in the house, but that won't stop him from finding them. She'll see him watching, but won't be able to do anything about it!

How's *that* for secret knowledge, Faith?

Milo smiles. He's going to see her naked a second time. Having sex! He can't *wait* to see the look on her face when she sees him wearing her bra and panties while watching them.

She will absolutely freak!

Jake finishes his shower, towels dry, walks past Faith's doorway wearing boxers. He enters his closet and puts on a pair of warm up pants, but remains shirtless.

Moments later the door beeps, and he hustles off to greet Faith.

Except that it's not Faith.

It can't be Faith because they're heading his way, toward the master bedroom. No way Faith would fuck Jake in the master bedroom knowing Milo's here.

He hears them enter the bedroom.

Jake says, "I can't believe you came."

She says, "We need to be quick."

Milo's face drops. A ball of ice forms in the pit of his stomach. It was only five words, but it was enough to make him retch. He covers his face with his shirt to keep the sound down while hearing Jake say, "Lift up your dress!"

Milo's not in the same room, so it's not like he could hear her perfectly when she said they needed to be quick. Sound's a funny thing. Maybe it caught him funny, maybe he was thinking about the party, or maybe he was still dazed and confused about whether to shoot Jake or not. God knows, he's been under an amazing amount of stress the last hour or so, and his mind could be playing tricks on him.

Just as he convinces himself that the woman lifting her dress up in the next room couldn't possibly, in a million years, be Lemon Fister, he hears her say, "Wait. Let me take it off completely. I can't go to my own birthday party with semen stains on my dress!"

"Good point," Jake says.

Milo waits a minute, then opens the door, walks a few steps, peeks around the corner, and watches his wife, Lemon Fister, getting thoroughly fucked by his friend, Jake Stallone. When it's over, she says, "Wait, I brought you something."

She reaches in her purse and pulls something out.

Jake laughs. "You've bought Milo another toothbrush?"

"I have. Do your thing."

"Are you sure?"

"Positive. It never gets old."

"Okay," Jake says. Then, to Milo's horror, he runs the bristles up his ass and hands her back the toothbrush.

"You know this is completely childish," Jake says.

"I know. But every time I watch him brush his teeth I crack up. Get it? Crack up?"

"You're terrible."

"I know. But Jake? Congratulations on winning the lottery. I'm really happy for you!"

"I won the lottery when I met you."

"That's sweet. Whose ticket is it? Yours or hers?"

"Hers."

"How do you know she bought one?"

"She always buys one, and always plays the same numbers. She's a creature of habit."

"Does she know?"

"Not yet."

"Maybe this will bring you and Faith closer together."

"Not a chance."

"Like you said, winning the lottery could change everything."

"There's something I never told you. Eight weeks ago Faith fucked a total stranger in the men's room of a bar."

"*What?*"

"I'm serious."

"Jake, that's crazy. She'd never do that."

"I *saw* her."

"What are you *talking* about? Where?"

"Cincinnati. I'd been at a client meeting, she was waiting for me in the hotel bar. I came in through the street entrance and saw her sitting at a booth, talking to a guy. I was so stunned, I watched them from a distance. After a few minutes they got up, went to the men's room. The fuckin' *men's* room!"

"That makes no sense. Of all the women I know—"

"Right. I know. But I was there. They stayed in the men's room more than five minutes. When they came out, they were all flushed."

"Did she see you?"

"No. She was too busy trying to fix her hair and smooth her clothes. She was following him very closely."

"I admit it sounds bad. But it doesn't prove they were having sex. Maybe he was selling her some coke. Or prescription pills."

"You're a good friend to assume that, but I listened at the door. She wasn't quiet, and she wasn't making drug deal sounds. They went back to the table a minute, then he left, and she went to the elevator. I knew she was up there changing her panties, so I went up to the room and waited for her to come out the door. When she did I told her I had to drop off my briefcase and pee. She went downstairs to get us a table, and I went through her suitcase and checked her panties for semen."

"Eew. Gross!"

"Yeah, I know. But it's not as gross as fucking a complete stranger in the men's room."

"Was there any?"

"Any what?"

"Uh...discharge?"

"Yeah. You couldn't miss it."

"Oh....My....God! Our Faith is a one-night-stander!"

"One-Night Faith."

"If I ask you something, promise not to get mad?"

"What?"

"How do you know he was a stranger?"

Jake pauses. "I guess I don't."

"You sound jealous."

"Not at all."

"You sure?"

"Of course. I've got you, right?"

She says, "I'm here, aren't I? When I'm supposed to be somewhere else?"

He kisses her boob.

She says, "What if she won't share the money?"

"She'll have to. And the minute she deposits the check, I'll file for divorce."

"Seriously?"

"Yes. And you will, too. Right?"

"You're asking me to take a big step without offering a proposal."

"Will you marry me?"

"For real? You mean it?"

"I do."

"Then yes, of course!"

"Happy birthday, baby."

"Thanks, sweetheart."

Milo watches them kiss, then trudges back to Faith's coat closet, with four things on his mind. One, he can't leave till Jake leaves, which will make him really late for Lemon's birthday party. Two, it's going to be a long-ass bike ride to his mom's house. Three, his wife's having an affair with his friend, and it's been going on for a while, or they wouldn't be talking marriage. And four, he's been brushing his teeth for months with toothbrushes that have spent a good amount of time up Jake's ass.

Chapter 7

BY THE TIME Milo arrives at Veluzzi's, the entire gang—
except for Jake—has been there a while. He catches Lemon's
cold look and Faith's questioning look at the same time and
ignores them both. He makes his way around the table, hugs
the women, and mumbles an apology about how his mom
had a rough afternoon.

Faith's face is pleading for confirmation the deed got
done, but Milo plans to let her stew a while, which is exactly
what she deserves for fucking a total stranger in a men's
room while chastising Milo for peeking at her body.

"Milo?" Lexi says. "I'd like to introduce you to my
friend, the incredibly good-looking Byron Zass. Byron, this is
Lemon's husband, Milo Fister."

Milo looks at Brody, who appears miserable to the point
of madness.

Milo shakes Byron's hand. "Pleased to meet you."

Lexi says, "Are you okay, Milo?"

"I'm fine. Just embarrassed being late for my wife's birthday party."

"No biggie," Lemon says. "Come sit. I've ordered you a drink."

He walks toward the empty seat beside his wife, notices the presents stacked on the floor. Says, "I'll be right back."

Lemon frowns. "What now?"

"I left your gifts in the trunk."

Faith says, "I'll help you fetch them!"

It came out so suddenly, everyone turns to look at her.

Faith recovers, saying, "I'd offer my husband, but as you can see, he's not here yet."

"I'll help you," Brody says.

"Thank you, Brody," Lemon says. Then looks at our friends and says, "I'm amazed Milo remembered my birthday at all!"

Right, Milo thinks. She's probably been telling their friends he's a rotten husband. Setting the stage for the "surprise" divorce that's coming his way. Of course, she'll lose all these friends when they find out she's been fucking Jake.

On the way to the car Brody says, "Lemon looks great tonight."

"You don't think her dress is a little wrinkled?"

Brody gives him an odd look. "I hadn't noticed." They walk quietly till he adds, "Are you gonna be in the doghouse tonight for being late?"

"Probably."

"I've never seen Lemon angry. But she looked upset with you tonight."

"Can you blame her? I was late for her party, after all."

"But your mom. Surely Lemon understands."

"She does. Still, it's her day. I should've been here."

They get the gifts out of the trunk. On the way back to the table Brody says, "What do you think of *Byron*?"

Milo says, "It had to happen, right?"

"I guess. But she just showed up with him, out of the blue. It sucks."

"It's been tough on you."

Brody nods.

Milo sees tears glistening in Brody's eyes. He says, "She'll never marry him."

"Why not?"

"Is his last name really Zass?"

"I doubt he'd make that up," Brody says.

"Lexi Zass?"

"What about it?"

"Say it quickly."

"What, "Lexi Zass?""

Milo smiles. "Sounds a lot like Lexi's *ass*, don't you think?"

Brody thinks about it and chuckles. "Good one." Then he says, "Milo?"

"Yeah?"

"Work on your marriage, okay? You don't want to wind up like me."

"You should bring someone next time."

"Fat chance."

Milo barely gets in his chair when Jake enters the room and says, "Looks like a *party*! Sorry I got tied up, but I wouldn't miss this for the world."

Over the next half hour Milo and Brody stare holes through Jake and Lemon, but neither can tell the two are even remotely interested in each other.

At one point Byron Zass says, "Milo, tell me something about Lexi I should know."

"She's faithful."

"Who isn't?" Jake says, looking at Faith.

"Who, indeed?" Faith says, returning the look.

Milo and Brody look at Lemon, but her expression gives up nothing. She says, "There's your answer, Byron. I suppose you'll never find a more faithful group of friends."

"Good to know," Byron says, showing Brody a winner's smirk. This, and the way Lexi blushes, tells everyone he and Lexi were seeing each other before she and Brody separated.

As for Jake and Lemon? Cool customers, these two. So cool Milo notices neither have said a word about Faith winning the lottery.

Then Jake does.

"I have a question for my lovely wife," he says. When she looks at him he asks, "Did you happen to buy a lottery ticket Thursday?"

She looks embarrassed, but says, "What if I did?"

"Did you play your favorite numbers?"

She frowns.

Jake says, "Ladies and gentlemen, if my wife played the numbers 11, 22, 33, 44, 55, with the powerball 17, as she always does, she just won $165 million dollars!"

They all look at Faith, but she doesn't see them.
She's already fainted.

Chapter 8

"YOU *SAW* HIM?" Faith says. "You saw Jake fucking Lemon? In our *home?*"

"Yeah. And it's been going on a long time."

They're at Starbucks. Faith's been here forty-five minutes, reading an electronic book, same as she does every Saturday morning while Jake hits the gym. He'll meet up with her at nine-thirty, give or take.

Creatures of habit, these two.

If it were Monday, she could just come to Milo's office. He's her attorney, after all. But it's Saturday, and the office is closed, so this is the best they could do.

Milo told her straight away about Lemon and Jake and said he could have filmed them if he hadn't left his phone at his mom's house.

At first, Faith refused to believe it. She cited the fact that Lemon and Jake barely acknowledge each other whenever they're in the same room. Then realized that piece of information was quite telling in its own right. Then she blew up and nearly made a scene.

After crying nonstop in the bathroom for fifteen minutes, Faith finally comes out and says, "I would've shot them both."

"I couldn't. All roads would lead back to me."

"I'm not going to share my money with that bastard."

"You won't have to."

"What do you mean?"

"I've found a killer-for-hire."

She lowers her voice to a whisper. "A *hit man?*"

"Hit woman, to be precise."

Faith regards him as she would a bug. "What would *you* know about locating a hit woman?"

"One of my clients knows a guy."

"That sounds sketchy. Who's your client?"

"I can't say."

"This sounds like one of those situations where you wind up in a car with a hidden camera recording your conversation."

"Are you sure there wasn't a hidden camera recording you in Cincinnati?"

"You've lost me."

"Eight weeks ago? Hotel bar in Cincinnati? Men's room?"

Her face flushes. "What are you *talking* about?"

"Jake told Lemon you fucked a complete stranger in the men's room."

"That's ridiculous!"

"He said he saw you talking, listened at the door, checked your panties for semen afterward. And found it."

She grits her teeth. "Tell me about the hit woman."

"This is the real deal. She's not cheap, but she's reliable."

"How much does she want?"

"Two-fifty."

Two hundred and fifty thousand dollars? Are you crazy?"

"It's that, or pay Jake $54 million to marry Lemon."

She says, "I'd rather have half the money than wind up in prison."

"I've already set up the meeting."

"You're joking."

"She wants two-fifty to kill one, three-fifty to kill both."

"I assume you're willing to chip in?"

"I didn't win the lottery," he says, and our ridiculous two-million-dollar house Lemon had to have is bleeding me dry. "But if you pay the two-fifty I can find a way to do the extra hundred."

"How do you know the hit woman's for real?"

"I asked her the same thing."

"And?"

"She said she'd prove it by killing someone we know that we don't care about."

"Excuse me?"

"That's what she said."

"And you said?"

"Byron Zass."

"Lexi's date?"

"The same."

"I don't understand."

"The hit woman's name is Maybe Taylor. If we decide not to use her I'll owe her fifty grand for the conversation. I assume you're willing to chip in?"

"No."

Milo frowns. "Why not?"

"You took it upon yourself to contact this killer. You took it upon yourself to have the conversation. You already owed her the money before talking to me. If we go forward, I'll be paying more than twice as much as you. And if we go forward, you won't have to pay the fifty in the first place."

He nods. "Okay."

She looks around. "What's this about Byron?"

I gave her his name. She said she'd kill him no later than Tuesday to prove she's for real."

"You believe her?"

"It makes sense. If she's secretly working for the cops, they'd never let her kill someone."

"We'd have to have proof Byron's dead."

"I told her that."

"Supposing she kills him. When would we meet her?"

"Friday morning."

"I've got spin class."

"What time?"

"Eight a.m."

"You can't cancel?"

"No. All the wives will be there. If I don't show up they'll come to my house to check on me."

Milo shakes his head. "It creeps me out to call this bitch. How about ten?"

"I can do ten."

"I'll call her."

"I'm not going to meet her without proof," Faith says.

"Me either."

PART TWO:
Callie and Creed

Chapter 1

STOMACH FLU'S A *bitch*, Callie thinks, clutching her tummy.

She falls to her knees, pukes on the hard wood floor of her penthouse condo. Tries to stand, but the cramping won't let her straighten up. Headache, faintness, vertigo, burning sensation in her throat and mouth...

...And something else.

The stench isn't right.

Gross, I know, she thinks, but sniffs her vomit anyway.

Something strange happening in her mouth. With hand under chin, she lowers her head, parts her lips, watches a steady drip of blood collect in her palm. When she spits, a tooth hits the pool like a stone, scattering the blood.

She blinks. Tries to comprehend what's going on, how it could have happened.

Her mind identifies the puke odor as bitter almonds.

She's been poisoned.

By whom?

Her husband, Donovan Creed.

Treatment? Antidotal therapy.

What she needs, and fast, is a Lilly cyanide kit: amyl nitrite, sodium nitrite, and sodium thiosulfate, with high-dose oxygen. No problem if she happened to be in or near a hospital. But she's trapped in her own home.

Without a phone.

Fitting way to end things, Callie thinks. She's poisoned plenty of others, knows what to expect. Convulsions. Respiratory depression. Pulmonary edema. Bradycardia. Paralysis. Coma. Death.

TV detectives smell a body and say, "Bitter almonds. Cyanide poisoning."

In the real world, hydrogen cyanide is virtually undetectable below 600 parts per billion. Callie can isolate the smell for two reasons. One, she's used the stuff often enough, and two, she's Callie: a woman with super hero powers of hearing and smell developed while catatonic as a child. To put it another way, if a gnat farts in LA, Callie can hear it in Vegas.

And smell it.

Not that this has been an advantage of living with a guy like Creed, who makes few apologies for bodily scents and sounds.

Speaking of which...

She opens her eyes. Sees Creed sleeping soundly in the bed beside her.

Creed the real-life boyfriend. Not the husband who poisons her in nightmares.

Callie has trust issues.

She sighs.

Creed opens his eyes.

"You okay?" he says.

"Sorry. Bad dream."

He studies her a moment. "Are you still angry about Kathleen?"

"What? Angry? Me?"

Chapter 2

Callie Carpenter.

AM I? CALLIE thinks. *Am I still angry about Kathleen meeting Creed for dinner last night?*

In a word, yes.

Kathleen Gray was Creed's first girlfriend since divorcing Janet, the nuclear hell bitch. She was also his first true love. They say the first real love lasts a lifetime, but after last night, Kathleen's life expectancy might be short enough to cause a blip in the insurance mortality table. Callie doesn't understand the attraction. In her mind, Kathleen's a dreary, clingy, needy, whiny bitch.

Not that Creed's other girlfriends were high on the food chain.

After Kathleen, Creed fell in love with the traveling freak show, Rachel Case. That was followed by a non-consummated close call with Beth Daniels, a widow he once referred to as "disarmingly attractive."

Disarminly attractive? What the hell does that mean?

Beth owns a bed and breakfast in St. Albans, Florida.

Disarming? I'll show her disarming! No arms would make her far less threatening.

There was also a brief dalliance with Miranda Rodriguez, one of New York City's finest.

Hookers, that is.

And who can forget the gorgeous Gwen Peters, who, until recently, was Callie's love interest?

But if Callie can only kill one of Creed's former girlfriends—and that's the legal limit, if she hopes to get away with it—she can't waste her kill. She needs to go after the biggest threat.

Is that person Kathleen?

Possibly not.

Kathleen's a former victim of spousal abuse. She's also a burn center volunteer, and the adoptive mother of a physically ill, emotionally-scarred child named Addie, who also attended Creed's surprise dinner last night.

Callie doubts Kathleen represents a serious threat to her future happiness.

Then again...you never know.

...Except that Callie *will* know...and soon.

Which brings us to Rachel Case.

Creed's soft spot for Rachel makes less sense than a Kardashian board meeting. She's currently locked away in a subterranean government facility having her eggs harvested by scientists who hope to create a Spanish Flu vaccine.

Jesus, Donovan.

Rachel Case?

How sick is this puppy? If a psychiatric scream mated with a jail-house sigh, their love child would be Rachel Case. What's that old Mickey Mouse joke? Oh yeah: Micky was mad at Donald Duck for spreading rumors about Minnie Mouse's sanity. Donald replied: *I never said Minnie was crazy. I said she was fucking Goofy!*

Well, Rachel's not fucking goofy. She's fucking crazy. If Creed goes back to her, Callie will kill *him* for bad judgment.

Which brings us to Beth Daniels.

Low level threat.

Classy? Sure. But Beth's lifestyle is too quiet for Creed. The most exciting part of her day is making toast, and her biggest decision is whether to butter it. What will she have him do, walk the beach and collect shells?

Please.

Callie might pay her a visit anyway, just to be safe. But Beth is almost certain to survive the cut.

The odds-on favorite to die is Miranda Rodriguez.

Unless Callie's meeting with Kathleen goes horribly wrong this afternoon, Miranda's holding the short straw.

Chapter 3

LAST NIGHT CREED attended a dinner meeting at the Four Seasons restaurant with Dr. Gideon Box. Concerned about a possible ambush, Creed called Callie on his cell phone and kept the line open so she could monitor the conversation. Callie positioned herself outside the entrance on East 52nd to provide backup should he need it.

It was an ambush, all right, but not the deadly kind. Unless Callie decides to kill Dr. Box for setting Creed up with Kathleen in the first place. Box met Kathleen while treating Addie and learned they had a mutual friend, Donovan Creed. Except that Kathleen hadn't been Creed's *friend*, she'd been his fiancée, and their relationship ended badly.

Homeland Security told Kathleen that Creed died in a terrorist firefight, and she believed it after attending his funeral. But years later she learned he was alive, living in Las Vegas. To Kathleen's credit, she never tried to contact him.

They'd been apart for years, and the implication was clear: he didn't want her, time to move on. But then Dr. Box started playing cupid, completely unaware Creed and Callie have become a couple.

She should kill him. Follow him home and fucking kill him.

Except that she owes Dr. Box, big time. He performed the surgery that gave Callie full use of her legs after a bullet crippled her.

Last night she listened as Creed approached the table and said, "Hello, Kathleen." Callie wasn't ready for that. Her brain cells spun like tumblers in a slot machine as she experienced the old emotions: Betrayal. Abandonment. Jealousy.

She wasn't mad at Creed. He'd been set up. She could tell from his voice he was upset at being ambushed by Kathleen and Addie. But he maintained his cool.

Because of Callie.

Because the dinner had been one of Box's conditions for performing Callie's operation.

Callie spent the first ten minutes fighting the urge to storm the restaurant and spray the table with bullets. Especially after hearing Kathleen's smartass comments and mocking tone.

The bitch was happier than a news crew at a plane crash! Everything about her voice suggested she wanted to have fun at Creed's expense. Clearly trying to make him feel uncomfortable, her first comment was characteristically bitchy: "Are you still dating Gwen Peters, the teenager?"

Creed said, "How'd you hear about Gwen?"

"Same way I hear about all your girlfriends: Amber Alerts."

"Funny," Creed said.

Then Addie, the little bitch in training, said, "What do you call a fish with no eyes?"

"I don't know. What?"

"A Fsh."

"A what."

"An F-s-h. Get it? No i's?"

"Right. That's funny. How have you been, Addie?"

"I'm good."

"Do you remember me at all?" he said.

"Not really. Mom said you almost married her when I was little. She said you were really nice to me, and helped take care of me."

"Well, you were a very special little girl."

"She still is, Donovan," Kathleen said.

You fucking bitch! He's trying to be nice. He got forced into this bullshit confrontation because he wanted to save my legs, and here you are, sticking it to him. Is that your plan, Kathleen? Seriously? You better hope you don't try to rekindle the relationship. Not tonight, and not ever. That would be a big mistake, because I don't play well. I don't share with others. Especially my lovers.

Creed knew Callie was listening. And fuming. After dinner, they met up in his limo, a block away, as planned.

"Sorry you had to hear all that," he said.

"You handled yourself well."

"I was afraid you'd be pissed."

"I am. But you had a worse time than me."

"Talk about awkward."

"Let's don't."

"Good idea."

What Callie didn't say is she left the restaurant ten minutes after Creed arrived. It's not like her to leave her post, but something came up. Something crazy. Something she has no plans of sharing with him.

She saw someone.

Walking down East 52nd.

Someone familiar.

A woman.

It was...Creed's former lover, Miranda Rodriguez. Miranda, who's supposed to be traveling in Europe for a year. Only she's not in Europe, she's in Manhattan.

And she's...

Pregnant.

Could Creed be the father?

Yes, of course he could. In fact, it's a certainty. Eight months ago Miranda agreed to come work for Creed, but insisted on taking a year off so she could travel Europe.

Now Callie realizes what the year was for.

She raced down the street to confront Miranda. Wanted answers, and wanted them badly. But something stopped her in her tracks.

Some unseen force.

She was completely conscious, completely alert, but her feet seemed stuck to the pavement. She saw Dr. Box's former nurse, Rose, staring at her.

Glaring at her.

Miranda looked concerned, but it didn't matter.

Callie couldn't move.

She heard thoughts in her head telling her to forget what she'd seen. The thoughts were powerful. Persuasive.

But Callie's dealt with mental demons her whole life. She knows how to isolate unwanted messages. She simply puts them in folders in her brain, to be opened in the future, or kept locked away forever.

When Rose and Miranda hurried away, Callie was unable to follow them.

At first.

Her field of vision was limited, so she couldn't tell if others noticed her predicament. Those who passed by her on the sidewalk seemed unaware of her presence.

Was she invisible?

A minute passed before the feeling came back. Callie took a few shaky steps, then raced to the corner where she last saw Miranda and Rose. Turned and ran several blocks, then retraced her steps, searching the stores. When she got back to the restaurant she realized what seemed like a half-hour was closer to three.

Though it wasn't easy, Callie survived the assault Rose made on her mind. And came away remembering Miranda's in Manhattan, pregnant, on the verge of giving birth.

To Donovan Creed's child.

A child that could destroy her relationship with Creed.

Except that...

The message in her brain was about more than just forgetting what she saw. It also included knowledge that Miranda isn't keeping the baby.

Rose is.

And Miranda won't even remember birthing a child.

All Callie has to do is keep the information to herself. Put it in one of her mental files and lock it away.

No problem.

No one on earth is better at hiding secrets than Callie.

Chapter 4

Donovan Creed.

I'M LOOKING AT the sexiest sight Planet Earth has to offer: Callie Carpenter, naked, in my bed.

Okay, so I'm exaggerating.

A little.

I mean, she *is* in my bed, and she *is* naked, but she's currently under the covers, which means it's not quite the sexiest sight a man can view.

Still, I know what you expect of me. It might make Callie angry, but I'm here for you. So hang on a sec while I—

"What' the *hell?*" Callie says.

I take it all in for you. Every curve, indentation, and both perfect protrusions. Then say, "I was just thinking the only thing sexier than lying beside you is seeing you naked."

She frowns, grabs the covers, pulls them back up.

"A minute ago you asked me about Kathleen, now you want to see me naked? Should I connect the dots?"

I laugh. "I asked if you were still angry that Dr. Box stuck me with Kathleen last night. Are you?"

Callie says, "It's over, right?"

"It's been over for years."

"So there's no reason for you to ever speak to her again?"

"No reason I can think of."

"Then no, I'm not angry."

Callie may not be angry, but I am. I tried to corner Dr. Box after the setup last night, but he scampered off when Addie gave me a hug. I chose not to chase after him and make a scene, but I probably should have, since I can't very well call the man while Callie's here.

My phone vibrates. I listen a minute, then hang up.

Callie says, "What's wrong?"

"Possible terrorist attack."

"Where?"

"Arkansas."

"Little Rock Air Force Base?"

"No."

"Pine Bluff Arsenal?"

"What's that?"

"Munitions storage."

"How do you *know* these things?"

"How do you *not*?"

"Willow Lake," I say. "It's a resort town in the Ozarks."

"It can't be tourist season there."

"No. The target appears to have been unoccupied vacation homes. The bombers purposely avoided population centers. If they wanted to kill large numbers of people they would've picked the town. Or an actual city. It'll be classified as a terrorist attack, but that definition doesn't pass the smell test. Not yet, anyway. It feels more like an attempted assassination. Or possibly—"

"—A test?" she says.

I nod.

"How bad was it?"

"Three witnesses, all shell-shocked, but no casualties. Numerous vacation homes leveled. It was definitely a military-style strike, with a two-phase bomb."

"That requires at least two people, right?"

"I think so."

"Then why are we sitting on our thumbs?"

"I'm part of the system now. I can't just sneak in and out. I have to wait for all the proper clearances."

"That sucks. But I'm going too, right?"

"I'd like you to."

"Then I'm going. Who else are we bringing?"

"Joe Penny."

She smiles. "You trust Joe above the government experts?"

"Not necessarily. But I can understand his explanations."

Forty minutes later we're on a jet helicopter awaiting takeoff when my phone rings. I check the caller ID and glance at Callie.

"Kathleen?" she says.

"Dani Ripper."

I notice a slight change in Callie's facial expression. I wouldn't call it a positive change.

She says, "What's Dani up to?"

I shrug, take the call.

Chapter 5

Callie Carpenter.

ANOTHER NAME FOR the list. Dani Ripper.

Callie doubts there's anything going on between Creed and Dani, but if something *is*, she wouldn't be the first woman to trust a man more than he deserved.

She hears Creed say, "Dani, I pride myself on always being available for you, but I'm kind of busy right now, unless your life's in danger."

What? He's always available for her? And prides himself on it?

Dani just made the endangered species list.

She hears him say, "I'll know more when we get there...Willow Lake, Arkansas. An entire neighborhood has just been blown off the map...We don't know. Are you in danger?"

He covers the phone and asks the pilots how long we have before takeoff. Then says, "I'm on the tarmac, waiting to taxi..."

He's on the tarmac? Not he and Callie?

"Just tell me what you need," Creed says. Dani says something, and Creed responds, "That's bullshit. We've been doing it for years...Homeland Security. CIA. FBI. The Pentagon. It's not that big a deal...No. these are classified programs...not if we erased them...Is that it?...No problem...You, too."

He hangs up, looks at Callie, and explains, "Dani had a technical question about erasing photos from cell phones."

"Photos of what?"

He shrugs. "I didn't ask."

The "You, too." bothers her. That's the last thing he said before hanging up. If someone on the other end of the phone ends a call by saying, "I love you," you'd respond, "I love you, too."

If you're free to speak.

But if you're unable to speak because your girlfriend is sitting next to you in a jet helicopter, you might respond, "You, too."

No sense asking him about it. If he's innocent it'll raise a red flag about her jealousy issues. And if he's guilty, she'll just be forcing him to lie. There are easier ways to determine if he and Dani are having an affair.

Torture comes to mind.

Chapter 6

Donovan Creed.

WE'RE FLYING TO Willow Lake with two pilots. Since only one is required to fly and land the chopper, I ask the copilot to take aerial photographs of the bomb site. As we approach the blast site, he directs the pilot to make a wide circle high above Leeds Road, then has him come closer, asks him to tilt, then make a tight circle.

After a few minutes, he turns to me and says, "We're done."

"Set her down, then," I say.

The pilot puts the chopper on the center of Leeds Road, midway between ground zero and the police road-block at Leeds and Route 53.

A young sheriff's deputy races toward us. When he finally arrives he tries to speak, but can't catch his breath. He puts his hands on his knees and pants like a dog.

"What's up, deputy?"

He takes a few more seconds to recover, then says, "Who am I talking to?"

"Donovan Creed."

"And you are?"

"I just *told* you. Donovan Creed."

"You can't be here, sir. This is Leeds Road. The bomb site's less than half a mile south." He points, in case I don't know which direction is south. As if I didn't survey the entire area before landing.

"Listen, son. We don't have time for bullshit. We've wasted hours obtaining proper clearance."

"No one told *me* about it."

"Sort of sad, isn't it? You do all the work but no one tells you anything? Get on the horn and tell them my name. Then tell me what I need to know. I saw two roadblocks, one on each end of the street."

"Road, sir."

"What?"

"We're on Leeds Road, sir."

I give him a look. "Are you fucking with me?"

"No, sir."

"Don't fuck with me son. I only saw one person at the blast site. That can't be right."

"There's just the one, sir. Everyone else is outside the roadblock, protecting the integrity of the scene."

"Integrity of the scene? Where'd you hear that?"

"Agent Phillips. FBI."

"FBI's here?"

"No sir, just Agent Phillips. But they're on the way. With a task force, a federal bomb squad, and all sorts of experts."

"That's us."

"You're the experts? From *Washington?*"

"That's right. I expect the president would want me to thank you for your dedication to duty."

"Wow!"

"Who's the guy I saw from the air? The one all alone at the blast site?"

"Agent Tyson Phillips, sir. He's FBI."

"You say that with reverence in your voice."

"Well, I mean, it's the *FBI!*"

"No one shits their pants any quicker."

"Sir?"

"I know for a fact the FBI doesn't have a field office in Willow Pointe."

"Willow Lake, sir."

"Whatever."

"Agent Phillips is from Little Rock. He was here, visiting his sister. He's been fielding questions, videoing the blast site, and live-streaming it to the task force."

"Live-streaming, huh?"

"Yes, sir. And preserving the scene till the task force arrives."

"With any luck we'll be gone before they get here."

He frowns. "The FBI's got full jurisdiction, sir. Agent Phillips has papers and everything."

"You can't be serious."

"FBI outranks us on this one. We were *bombed!*"

"What's this guy's title?"

"Tyson Phillips? He's an FBI attorney."

"Shut *up*!"

"Sir?"

"Do you mean to stand there and tell me your dynamic Willow Pointe police force is sucking hind tit to an FBI *attorney*?"

"Willow Lake, sir. And yes, they said he's in charge. I mean, he's FBI, and all."

"Did he show you his ankle holster?"

The deputy looks confused. "How'd you know?"

"They're awfully proud of that ankle holster. Never miss a chance to let you know they're packing. "

The deputy looks at Callie and Joe Penny, then back at me. "Who *are* you guys?"

"Homeland Security. And before you go all FBI on me again, you should know that the droppings in my *parakeet* cage outrank Agent Phillips. He and the Feebs can take their photos and soil samples and core borings and all the other cluster fuck bullshit we pay them to do. If they stay out of my way, I'll even let them take the credit for solving the case. But the three of us are here to determine two things: Was this a terrorist act? And if so, is the country in danger?"

"You think it is?"

"I don't know, but I intend to find out."

He looks like he's about to trust us. Then a funny look crosses his face. He says, "You're not reporters, are you?"

"Do we look like reporters?"

"You look like movie stars. You and her, anyway."

Joe Penny says, "Not me?"

Callie says, "Mr. Creed already told you we're with Homeland Security. Up to now, we've been polite. But you need to let us do our jobs."

The deputy looks skeptical. "Do you have any credentials?"

I briefly consider killing him, but he's a young guy, just doing his job. I respect that. But I can tell Callie's itching to snuff him, so I ask her to show him our paperwork. She does, and he finally turns and starts trotting back to his post. Callie, Joe, and I head south, to the blast site. As we begin picking our way through the rubble, FBI Agent Tyson Phillips shouts, "Halt! Do not take another step!"

Callie says, "I'll get this."

She peeks into her handbag, then strolls over to him, shows him our paperwork. Unfortunately, he's having none of it, so she kicks him in the nuts, clubs the back of his neck, and he goes down face first. She puts a knee in the center of his back, pulls his arms toward her, and handcuffs him with two plastic zip ties. He starts hollering his disapproval, so she rolls him over and knocks him unconscious. Then removes his shoes and socks and stuffs the socks in his mouth and tapes his lips shut. While waiting for him to regain consciousness, she tapes his ankles together.

Then she walks back to where we're standing and says, "That ought to hold him."

"What type of tape did you use?"

"Filament."

Joe says, "Are we gonna get in trouble for this?"

"Probably," I say. "But it couldn't be helped. He wasn't going to give us access, and Callie saved him from getting shot."

"You would've *shot* him?"

"He probably would have shot himself, trying to grab his gun. But yeah, I would've shot him. If this is the first wave of a terrorist attack we need to put jets in the air. We can't fuck around with these paper-pushers."

Joe Penny's my bomb-builder and expert of choice. But lately I've noticed serious flaws in his character, like compassion and empathy. Not to mention he's questioned my judgment several times on this trip. Worst of all, he's crushing on Callie, big time.

On the plus side, Joe's an artist. He builds special-purpose bombs that distract or kill with surgical precision. When it comes to tactical work, he's the best.

I use other bomb-builders, of course. You know, for mass-murdering. When I need massive explosions, I don't require a specialist like Joe. I simply look for a guy with goats in his yard.

If Joe wants to keep breathing for an extended period of time he'll have to find a way to overcome his lust for Callie. In the meantime, he's on my payroll. In fact, he's the only munitions expert I keep on salary. The balance of my staff is comprised of assassins and researchers, and I've got the best of both.

The assassins are exactly what you'd expect, including Maybe Taylor, who happens to be my daughter. But my research team would surprise you. It's comprised of three celibate males, Curly, Larry, and C.H., who are, respectively, a midget, a dwarf, and an elf.

These three vertically-challenged geniuses work and live in Geek City, a protected area of the Sensory Resources complex. My offices are in the same complex, different annex. Sensory Resources is a clandestine branch of Homeland Security, whose prime directive is identifying domestic terrorists and killing them before they have a chance to carry out attacks. Ninety-nine percent of our work is done quietly, behind the scenes, so I don't normally require clearance. When I do, it's hard to come by, since only a handful of people know about Sensory Resources, and even fewer know I'm the newly-appointed director of the agency. Since we don't technically exist, we have to pose as Homeland Security bigwigs.

Now, at ground zero, I'm impressed by the extent of the damage. Portions of doors, toilets, appliances, flooring, and sections of staircases are still intact, but nothing—from walls to fireplaces—remains vertical. The target and the surrounding homes are basically rubble.

"I can't believe no one was killed," I say.

"What do we know about the survivors?" Callie asks.

"Sheriff Cox will have to brief us."

Joe says, "You'd think the place would be crawling with cops and gawkers by now."

"This is a small, secluded town. A resort area. Most of these lake homes are vacant. When terrorists attack, people tend to hide till they know it's safe to come out. The blast occurred hours ago, but if you heard a terrorist bombed a small town in Arkansas, wouldn't you stay away?"

"Not me!" Joe says.

"Well, me either. But most people would."

It takes us thirteen minutes to conclude three things: One, the blast was the result of a domestic terrorist attack featuring a two-step bombing. Two, the main target was the second home on the block, which we already know was owned by a man named Jack Russell, the alias of bounty hunter Jack Tallow. Three, Tallow's lake house had a secret room.

Callie says, "Bingo."

She holds up a chunk of wood.

"What's that?"

"Top piece of an interior door."

"And that's significant because?"

She smiles. "There's a phone number written on it."

"*What?*"

"A phone number. Written by a woman. Now tell me I'm good."

"You're *damn* good!"

I pick my way over to her and study the chunk of wood. Joe follows me and says, "Why would someone write a phone number on the top edge of a door?"

"Because no one would think to look for it there."

"But *you* did."

"Yeah, but I'm good."

"How do you know it was written by a woman?"

"It's distinctively feminine."

"Maybe Agent Phillips wrote it," I say.

Callie laughs.

Joe says, "That phone number could be ten years old."

"It could be an old number," I say. "But according to Jack's toilet, the message is less than a year old."

"You talk to toilets?" Joe says, giving Callie a wink.

There it is again. Like every man on earth, Joe finds Callie impossibly attractive. When men see good-looking women their first thought is *I wonder if she might be interested in me.* Joe's testing the water. He's thinking he and Callie are young, I'm older. Maybe that's an angle he can exploit. Needling the boss a bit, putting me down in front of Callie makes him appear cool. He probably hopes they'll get some banter going at my expense.

I can't blame the kid for trying, but Callie's way out of his league. And if he's trying to impress her he's going about it the wrong way, because Callie respects me. By poking fun at me, arguing with me, questioning my judgment, he's coming dangerously close to disrespecting me. Callie would never tolerate that. It's the sort of thing that would cause her to rise to my defense. Joe doesn't get that, but again, he's young. He might be skilled with conventional explosives, but in my experience nothing's more combustible than a strong-willed woman. And Callie's more explosive than any bomb Joe will ever create. I expect she'll deal with his impertinence, if he crosses the line. In the meantime, maybe I can work in a little bit of teaching.

I say, "All houses talk, Joe. You just have to know how to listen. We stepped over a toilet lid a minute ago."

"So?"

"Toilet lids are stamped with the date of manufacture."

"Maybe it was a new toilet lid."

Callie and I look at each other. She says, "If he's getting on your nerves, I've got plenty of tape left."

Joe looks at her with wounded surprise.

Callie and I type the phone number into our cell phones and walk to an area free from debris.

"What about Agent Phillips?" Joe says.

"He'll be fine."

"Won't the FBI be pissed when they find him bound and gagged?"

"I hope so."

I dial my research team at Sensory. Larry, the dwarf answers. I tell him to turn down the music that's blaring in the background. When he does, I give him the number Callie found on the door and tell him to locate the signal.

Four minutes later he calls me back and says the phone in question is at or beside a hotel in Memphis, Tennessee, less than a mile from the international airport.

"How long has it been there?"

Larry puts me on hold. A few minutes later he puts me on speaker and says, "Nine hours, give or take."

"And before that?"

"I bet the others fifty dollars you already know."

"Willow Lake."

"Come to papa!"

"Not so fast!" C.H. says. "Ask him who it belongs to!"

I say, "Right now all I've got is the belief it belongs to a woman."

"Crap!" Larry says.

In the background I hear C.H. and Curly laughing heartily, which means they're probably dancing a jig. It's absurd, I know, but when you're dealing with the world's greatest researchers, that's what you have to do: deal with them.

"Call the hotel," I say. "Find out who checked in nine hours ago. There won't be many at that time of the morning, and probably just our lady. I want her name and room number."

"They won't want to give us that information."

"Use your imagination."

"Can we threaten the front desk lady with bodily harm? Like in the movies?"

"No."

"Why not?"

"You won't scare her. No offense, but you're elves."

"One elf. At most."

"Nevertheless, your voices aren't threatening. I know you wish they were, but they're not. On the other hand, you're government elves. Threaten her with a tax audit. After you get her name and room number, call one of our Memphis agents and have him stand outside her hotel room door. No one leaves the room till I say so."

"Mr. Creed?"

"What?"

"We don't have any agents in Memphis."

"Why not?"

"You haven't recruited any."

"We've got drivers there, right?"

"Several."

"Good. Get the biggest, toughest, most intimidating guy we've got, and tell him to get there immediately. Tell him she can't leave the room under any circumstances. When everything's in place, give me a call."

"What if she's already gone?"

"Keep an eye on the tracer. If the phone moves, I want the driver close behind."

Chapter 7

CALLIE, JOE, AND I make our way to the roadblock, south of the blast site, where 20 men have gathered around the sheriff. I don't know if they came to protect him, or the crime scene, or if they just wanted to be here when the FBI taskforce shows up. But whatever their reason, it's been forgotten, now that Callie's in their presence.

All eyes are on her like maggots on a corpse.

I flash my badge at Sheriff Cox, but he says that's not good enough. It could be a fake. I won't argue the point, because in fact, it *is* a fake. Sensory Resources doesn't issue badges. But we *do* have valid credentials, and Callie produces them. Sheriff Cox pretends to study them carefully before answering my questions, but what he's really studying is the lower half of Callie's anatomy.

Now that we're dating, and planning to live together, I need to ask her to stop wearing camel-toe jean tights, or leggings, or whatever the hell they're called.

When he's done ogling her, I ask, "Was a woman staying at Jack's house?"

"How'd you know?"

"We've got a top-flight research team."

"You've seen her picture?"

"No."

"She's damn good-looking." He gives Callie another quick mental undressing and adds, "Not compared to you, Miss Carpenter."

Callie shows him a smile so radiant it catches him off-guard. His knees buckle. He nearly goes down.

I get it.

She's dazzling.

Normally I'd let Callie's flirting work its magic, but right now I'm not in the mood.

I'm pissed.

Not only that, but I'm pissed that I'm pissed. What I'm saying, I'm shocked to realize it matters to me that this jackass is molesting my girlfriend with his eyes. And I'm furious at myself for having this weakness. When you're in my business, playing at my level, the thing that kills you is your soft spot. Your weakness. You simply can't survive long when they learn about your weakness.

"The woman's name?" I say, making an effort to hold my temper.

He answers me while staring at Callie. "She was going by Emma Wilson, but when I ran her ID it came up identity theft. The real Emma died twenty-one years ago in a car crash. I don't know if the phony Emma killed Jack Russell, or was just using him, but she had his house key, credit card, and a stack of cash that likely belonged to him. She took off shortly before the blast."

"Who saw her last?"

"Millie Reston."

"Where's she?"

"In there with the others," he says, pointing to a nearby tent.

"What others?"

"The BWC's."

Callie looks at me, then says, "We're not familiar with that term."

"Normally I'd keep this confidential," Sheriff Cox says. "But we're a small town, and I'm not the one who found them. So basically, the whole town knows the story."

"Except for us," Callie says.

His eyes go straight to the swell of Callie's breasts, and eventually her face. "You're that movie star, right?"

"You know I'm not. You've seen my papers. But thanks for the compliment. What's a BWC?"

"We don't know. It was written on the asses—pardon my French—of the three victims."

"Victims?" I say. "We were told there were no casualties."

"You were told right. No one died. But a young man and two women were in the general blast area. They were knocked down, disoriented. Some fella came running up from the lake, pulled their pants down, and wrote BWC on their asses with a grease pen."

"Makes sense."

"It *does*?"

"No, of course not."

"I don't understand."

"Let's just say comedy ain't easy, and leave it at that. So what does BWC stand for?"

"We don't know."

"You've had hours to think about it."

"Maybe it's the bomber's initials."

"That'd be pretty stupid, don't you think?"

He shrugs.

Callie says. "What else can you tell us?"

"There was a homicide a few hours before the blast. Local guy named Darryl Rhodes. Jack Russell had been banging Darryl's wife, Abbey."

"Abbey Roads?" Callie says. "Like the Beatles?"

"What beetles?"

Callie stares at him blankly.

He says, "Emma was staying at Jack's house, posing as his fiancée. Darryl came over with the intention of raping her."

"Why?"

"Because of Jack's affair with Abbey."

"Charming."

"Darryl was about to get violent when someone—not Emma—shot him from the hill across the street."

I try to piece it together. "The bombing occurred several hours *after* the homicide?"

"That's right. We spent hours working the Darryl Rhodes homicide. When we'd done all we could, we cordoned off the area and everyone went home. Moments later, the bombs went off. It was like he was waiting for everyone to leave."

"The grease pen guy?"

"Yeah."

"Anyone get a good look at him?"

"No. It was dark, and like I said, the three that may have seen him were disoriented."

"You think the grease pen guy had something to do with the bombs?"

"I do. But he wasn't flying the crop duster."

"You've lost me."

"Witnesses saw a crop duster flying over the lake, heading toward Leeds Road. That's rare for nighttime, so they kept watching and saw the pilot drop some sort of dust bomb. Then a missile of some kind flew up from the lake and exploded in the middle of the first bomb."

"Then what happened?"

"All hell broke loose."

"Anyone seen Jack?"

"We haven't been able to locate him, but it turns out he was using an alias, too. His real name is—"

"Jack Tallow. I know. Thanks, Sheriff."

"Where are you going?"

"To the tent."

"The FBI told us to wait till they get here before questioning the BWC's."

"Sounds like good advice."

Callie and I show our credentials to the deputy guarding the tent, and he goes through the process of pretending to study them while scoping out Callie's crotch. I swear, her pants are annoying the shit out of me, even though I'm enjoying the view as much as anyone.

The three of us go in the tent and I tell Joe to remove everyone except the cute twenty-year-old girl.

"Where should I take them?"

"Stand with them outside the tent. We'll call you in a minute."

Joe escorts five people out, leaving Callie and me with the young lady.

"What's your name?"

"Abbey Rhodes." She, too, checks out Callie's lower half. Then says, "You ain't from around here."

"Sadly, no," Callie says.

"Where'd you get them pants?"

"They're not pants," Callie says. "It's spray paint."

"No shit? You just sprayed paint on your legs?"

Abbey practically puts her face in Callie's crotch to get a closer look. As she does so, Callie smiles at me to prove how easy it is for her to get female attention. Trying to make the point if I want her to be faithful I need to stay on my toes.

Callie says, "You're not related to the Rhodes Scholarship folks, are you?"

"No ma'am."

"What a shock."

I say, "Abbey, I understand someone wrote some letters on your backside."

"Some asshole, you mean. What about it?"

"Show us."

"Fuck you!"

Callie's body and hands become a blur. She drops into a crouch and jabs her thumb and forefinger deep into Abbey's stomach. As Abbey starts to double over in pain, Callie unbuttons her jeans, pulls them down to her knees, along with her panties. By then, Abbey's torso has fallen onto Callie's shoulder. Callie stands, and holds Abbey over her shoulder like a fireman rescuing a woman from a burning building.

The entire procedure took less than two seconds!

The fact that Abbey's quite pretty has nothing to do with how carefully I inspect her ass. And the longer I stare, the harder she kicks. She's seconds away from getting her breath back, at which point she'll probably scream.

"Getting an eye full?" Callie says, with great annoyance.

"Let's change places."

We do, and Callie sees what I saw: a helluva nice ass with no writing on it.

No initials, no grease residue, no marks of any kind.

I can't blame Abbey for being mad. On the other hand, I did ask her nicely to show us her ass. Even Callie would admit that.

I lower her from my shoulder so she can stand comfortably, and sidestep her attempt to kick my shin. She takes a deep breath, preparing to scream, but just before the sound comes, I say, "If you're about to scream, pull your pants back up so the others won't see you naked."

It takes her a second to realize her pants are still around her knees. She pulls them up. Then—without so much as a thank you for protecting her modesty—she screams bloody murder. Callie grabs her throat and gives it a pinch.

The screaming stops.

As people come pouring into the tent, Callie whispers something into Abbey's ear. I frown at Joe for letting the deputies and others get past him, but he's just a kid. A bomb-builder, not an assassin. If they *knew* he was a bomb-builder they'd fear him. But you know what they say about "if." —If your aunt had wings and a nut sack she'd be your uncle, in heaven.

"What the hell's going on here?" the deputy yells.

Abbey tries to speak, but her voice won't cooperate. Finally she squeaks, "Everything's fine. I just had a flashback to when Darryl got shot."

I ask, "Who else had grease marks on their butts?"

A woman and a young man raise their hands.

"You're Millie Reston?"

She nods.

I look at the kid. "Who are *you?*"

"Ellwood Fillmore. My parents own Fillmore's Grocery."

"Abbey washed the evidence off her backside," I say. "What about you guys?"

"I did too," Millie says. "No one told us it was evidence."

I look at Ellwood. "And you?"

"Hey, if it ain't Saturday, I don't bathe."

"Well, hey, Ellwood," I say, pointing at his pants. "Since it ain't Saturday, shuck 'em."

"What? Right here? In front of everyone?"

"No. Just me and the blonde. Everyone else out. Now!"

When they leave, Ellwood asks what right we have to make him strip. Callie takes care of it by telling him he's a hero. Says his ass could save the country from terrorism. He reluctantly removes his pants, and sure enough, the letters BWC are written on his ass. Callie and I take pictures with our cell phones. Then mine rings, and Larry the dwarf tells me a woman named Emma Wilson checked into the airport hotel in Memphis just after 3:00 a.m. She's in Room 232, and so is her phone.

"Our driver will be there in ten minutes," Larry says.

I hang up and tell Callie and Joe we need to hustle back to the chopper.

"We're going to Memphis?" Callie says.

"We are."

"I had plans for this afternoon."

"What time?"

"Two o'clock, give or take."

"You might need to postpone."

"I'd rather not."

I know better than to ask Callie about her plans. We're determined not to have that type of relationship. So I say, "I'll have the chopper drop me off in Memphis, then you and Joe can take it back to New York City."

"I'd like to get back to Vegas," Joe says.

"Fine. You can catch a commercial flight out of Memphis."

He says, "You want to hear my take on the explosion?"

"Of course."

The crop duster was equipped with a conventional ex-plosive. Probably a canister that fit in the cargo bay. They rigged a trap door, pressed a button, dropped the payload. Then used a scatter charge to detonate it."

"Sheriff said it was a dust bomb."

"The canister was filled with powdered aluminum."

"Why?"

"The first explosion created a mushroom cloud of aluminum powder. Then the grease guy fired a thermobaric warhead from the ground into the cloud."

"To enhance the explosion?"

"Right."

Callie says, "Why not just drop a bigger bomb from the crop duster?"

Joe says, "They probably just had the one crop duster, and needed the two-step process to do enough damage."

"But they didn't kill anyone."

"Only because they didn't want to."

"So it's not a terrorist attack," Callie says.

"I think it was," I say. "Just not a conventional one."

She stops walking a moment, so Joe and I stop. Then she says, "You should be relieved, but you're not. You look concerned. Why?"

"I'm getting a really bad feeling about this."

"Why?"

"The writing."

"BWC?"

I nod.

Joe's look says he thinks I'm crazy. "Someone detonated an FAE over a civilian neighborhood and the part that bothers you is three people got grease on their asses?"

"That's right."

"Why?"

Callie looks at me, then Joe, and says, "It's a Monty Python."

Joe says, "What's a Monty Python?"

"Something completely different."

"It fits no profile," I explain. "This was a test of some sort. An attention-getter."

"Which means?"

"Something big's about to happen. And the letters are a clue."

We start moving again. After a few minutes we pass Agent Phillips, who's rolling around on the ground, glaring at us. Joe nods at him, as if apologizing.

Callie says, "There were three people with writing on their asses."

"What about it?"

"What made you pick the young, pretty one?"

"I planned to photograph all three asses."

"But you started with hers. Why?"

"Of the three, I figured Abbey would make the biggest fuss about stripping. If we saved her for third, she would've known what was coming. She would've thrown a fit. You know how cops are with locals. They would have insisted we didn't have the right to pull her pants down."

Joe says, "They'd have been right."

"For a bomb builder, you're an odd duck," I say.

No one responds or comments, so we walk quietly for several minutes. As we near the chopper I ask, "What did you whisper to Abbey to make her stop screaming?"

"I told her if she kept her mouth shut I'd kill Emma Wilson for her.'"

"Brilliant."

"Thanks."

I pause a minute, then say, "But you can't kill her. You know that, right?"

"We'll see," Callie says.

We climb in the chopper, take our seats. While awaiting lift-off, I eye Callie carefully. It doesn't take much to set her off, and I hadn't noticed it before, but she's clearly on edge about something. While Callie's not the only person on earth with bi-polar issues and a hair-trigger personality, she's quite unique in how she expresses displeasure.

What I'm saying, when Callie gets like this, people die.

"Everything okay?" I ask.

"Peachy," she says.

Chapter 8

Jill Whittaker.

JILL'S CELL PHONE is ringing?

Not possible.

Is it?

She answers, "Jack? Please tell me it's you!"

"It's me. What's up?"

Shit, she thinks. Then says, "Who *is* this? How'd you get my number?"

"It's Jack. Talk to me."

"Look, asshole. First of all, Jack doesn't sound like a cartoon character. Second—"

"Yeah?"

She hangs up. No point in continuing the conversation. Whoever called obviously found her number on the top edge of the bathroom door where she left it for Jack.

How the hell did the door survive the blast?

And how could she let herself think for one minute Jack escaped? And how could she expect him to talk to her after Bobby cut out his vocal cords?

Simple. She thought those things because she *wanted* to. Because she's an optimist. And because hope springs eternal.

But this is the real world. If Bobby claimed he removed Jack's vocal cords, then Jack will never speak again, period. Not that it matters, since Jack's either dead or soon will be.

It's not that she loves Jack. She barely knows him. But she does feel responsible. That said, she needs to move along. Needs to take care of herself. Needs to get as far away from her crazy husband, Bobby, as possible.

Ryan Decker, the terrorist, went to a great deal of trouble to help her. He lied for her. Told Bobby she died in the explosion. Then gave her a ride to Memphis.

She should have ditched her phone in the lake last night, but she kept it, hoping the information she heard about Jack was wrong. By answering her phone just now, Bobby's goons have learned she's alive.

Assuming the call was made by one of Bobby's goons.

But what if it wasn't?

She presses the redial button.

"You're right," the voice says. "I'm not Jack. I'm Donovan Creed, with Homeland Security. I found your number on a piece of wood at a blast site. Who am I talking to?"

Jill hangs up. The good news is Bobby doesn't know she survived the blast. The bad news is it wasn't Jack who found the number.

The phone rings again.

They're probably trying to trace it. Get her on the line, keep her talking. On TV when the suspect calls, the screen starts with a map of the U.S. and keeps updating to a region, then a state. On TV there are lots of glowing, pulsing signals. On TV the tracer guy says, "Keep her talking. We're almost there! Another ten seconds and—" But then the suspect hangs up and the screen goes black. Never fails. Somehow the TV villains always know just how long it takes the cops to triangulate the location of the cell phone. Does that mean if she doesn't answer, they won't be able to find her?

Wait.

Donovan Creed's in Willow Lake, Arkansas, and she's in Memphis, Tennessee. So even if he traces her phone, she'll have plenty of time to get away. She's on foot, but men like her. She can catch a ride with someone in the lobby or parking lot. And if not, she can take the shuttle to the airport, which is just across the interstate.

The point is, Jill can safely take the call. If she wants to.

Does she?

The phone stops ringing.

Should she wait till it rings again, or call back?

She presses the redial.

Creed answers. "Should I call you Emma?"

"That'll work. For now."

"Emma, I need your help."

"What's in it for me?"

"What do you want?"

"Are you kidding? I'm a woman."

Creed chuckles. "Good answer. How much do you know about the bombing at Willow Lake?"

"Everything."

"Perfect! Start at the beginning. Leave nothing out."

"Sorry, pal. I don't have that much time. But I'll tell you the basics if you'll do two things for me."

"Name them."

"I want you to rescue Jack Tallow."

"Where is he?"

"Have you heard of Bobby DiPiese?"

"Bobby Dee? The mob boss? Yeah, sure. What about him?"

"He's got a basement dungeon in his home, near La Pierre, Louisiana. Jack's being held prisoner there, along with a bunch of others. You'll recognize Jack right away. He's the one who can't talk."

"Why can't he talk?"

"Because Bobby cut his vocal cords out."

"And you know this because?"

"The terrorist told me."

"The one who blew up Jack's lake house?"

"Yup."

"You called him a terrorist, not a bomber, or dissident."

"That's how he identified himself. He said he's an urban terrorist."

"What's his name?"

"I'll tell you when you rescue Jack."

"Consider it done. I'll call you back as soon as I hear something."

"Don't. I'm ditching this phone. But give me your number and I'll call you tomorrow. Save Jack, and I'll give you the guy's name and physical description."

"Why should I believe you possess that information?"

"You'll have to trust me."

"You're putting my life in danger with Bobby Dee and giving me nothing in return."

"You'll get what you want when I get what I want."

"Tell me something I don't already know. Just to whet my appetite."

"Okay. I'm great in bed."

Creed laughs. "I knew that already."

"No you didn't."

"You had Jack's house, credit card, and a huge stack of cash. You survived a physical assault from Darryl Rhodes and a bombing that leveled half the neighborhood."

She laughs. "All of which tells you I'm good in bed?"

"The evidence screams it."

"Well, how can we argue against the evidence?"

"We can't. So tell me your real name."

"Ask me something else."

"The guy that fired the missile from the lake. The terrorist."

"What about him?"

"He wrote BWC on the bodies of three survivors."

"So?"

"Any idea what it means?"

"If I tell you, will you promise to rescue Jack?"

"Does it count if he's dead?"

"No."

"If he's alive, I'll rescue him. If not, I'll recover him."

"Because we can."

"Excuse me?"

"That's what BWC stands for."

"*Because we can?* What does that mean?"

"I'm not sure. But Ryan says it's going to be a household saying."

"Ryan?"

"That's his first name."

"When's he planning to strike?"

"Soon."

"Shit."

"Save Jack. I'll call you tomorrow."

"Emma?"

"Yeah?"

"I *will* find Jack. But hang onto your phone."

"Why?"

"Because you're at the airport hotel, Memphis, Tennessee, Room 232, and I've got an agent stationed outside your door. You're not going anywhere till I get there. You're going to help your country find this prick, Ryan, and I'll make it worth your while by keeping you out of prison."

She hangs up, runs to the door, opens it, sees a giant man standing there.

He smiles. "Hi Emma."

She does a double-take.

Then smiles back and says, "I'll be damned! Frank Sturgis."

He says, "What are the chances?"

They hug.

She says, "You still driving the cab?"

"I am. And you're still on the run?"

"Yup. Give me a lift?"

"Let's talk a minute first."

"I'm in a bit of a hurry."

"I know. But you may be in over your head this time. Can I tell you why?"

"Okay. But afterward, if I still want a ride?"

"I'll take you where you want to go."

"Thanks, Frank."

As they enter her room his phone rings. He listens a while, then says, "Yes sir."

When he hangs up, she asks, "Was that Donovan Creed?"

Frank nods.

"Is he really with Homeland Security?"

"Not exactly. But he kills terrorists for them."

"But you can handle him."

"No one can handle Creed. He's the most dangerous person on earth."

"You're exaggerating. I just spoke to him twice. He's all talk."

"When Creed's in Pamplona, the bulls run from *him*."

She stares at him a minute. "I don't have any idea what that means."

"It means, don't fuck with him."

She laughs.

"I'm serious, Emma."

"Call me Jill."

"Why?"

"It's my real name."

He nods. "Thanks for sharing that. From what I gather, you've had quite a week."

"Can I be frank?"

"No. I'm Frank."

"Funny. But yeah, you might say I've had a rough week. I've been drugged, bound, robbed, kidnapped, and attacked by four drunken gay deer hunters. I escaped, met you, and you drove me to Willow Lake, where I was physically attacked by a 300-pound redneck who was suddenly murdered five feet from me by a terrorist hired by the mob to blow me up. He did, in fact, blow up the entire neighborhood, but as you can see, I managed to escape."

"And here you are."

"Yes. So I think I can handle a bureaucrat like Donovan Creed, who talks like a cartoon character."

"Creed's no bureaucrat. And the cartoon voice is an imitation."

"Of what?"

"It's a quirk. Whenever he tries to imitate someone, or disguise his voice, it comes out like Sponge Bob."

"You're joking."

"Like I say, it's a quirk."

"And I'm supposed to fear this man?"

"Beyond all others."

She thinks a minute. "Is it your opinion he could take down Bobby Dee?"

"Without batting an eye."

"You're serious?"

"Completely."

Jill grins, grabs her phone, presses the redial button.

"How's Frank treating you?" Creed says.

"No complaints. But it dawns on me I never told you my second demand."

"Then tell me something else I don't already know."

"My maiden name's Jill Whittaker. But don't waste your time writing that down."

"Too late. Thanks, Jill."

"My married name is DiPiese. I'm Bobby's wife."

"Holy shit!"

Jill smiles. "Thought you might like that."

Frank doesn't. His eyes have gone huge.

Creed says, "The folks at Willow Lake will be surprised. They thought Jack was your fiancée."

"That was our cover story, so I could stay at his place."

"What do I owe you for the information?"

"I want you to kill Bobby."

"When?"

She laughs. "I love that. You said when, not why. We're going to get along swimmingly, Donovan. Not that it matters, but are you good-looking?"

"Yeah, but not by choice. My face has been reconstructed."

"You don't strike me as a vain man."

"I won't strike you at all, if you behave."

"How good do I have to be?"

"Don't flirt. I'm spoken for."

"Pity."

"I'm still 30 minutes out, but I've called a sketch artist who should be there in a few minutes. I'd like you to start without me. That way we can get the terrorist's face in front of the public within the hour."

"That's not going to happen. Frank and I will be gone by then."

Creed pauses a moment, then says. "You really *must* be good in bed! I'm impressed. On the other hand, I'm deeply disappointed in Frank. Have a safe trip, Jill."

"I must say, you're being an awfully good sport about this."

"I'm a realist. I'm only sorry you'll miss the reunion."

"Which reunion is that?"

"I found Jack Tallow. I thought you might want to see him."

Jill closes her eyes. "If you found him this quickly he's obviously dead."

"Actually, he's alive and in deep shit with the Baton Rouge police department."

"You've clearly found the wrong Jack Tallow."

"You think? Let's review. The Jack Tallow I've found has no vocal cords and is sporting savage, near-fatal hog bites."

"Thank God!" she says.

"You're happy about the hog bites?"

"Yes, of course. It means he escaped. He said he would, and he did. Why's he in trouble with the cops?"

"I'll tell you when I get there."

Chapter 9

Donovan Creed.

WHEN WE LAND in Memphis I kiss Callie goodbye and keep Joe with me, so he can blow up Bobby Dee's house in La Pierre, Louisiana, later tonight.

Before catching a cab I find a quiet spot and call Dr. Box's cell phone.

No answer.

I call his apartment.

Bingo.

A young woman with a thick southern drawl says "Hi there! Who's callin'?"

I can actually *feel* the smile in her voice. If I weren't so pissed at Dr. Box, I'd smile back. "I'm Donovan Creed."

"Well, hey there, Mr. Creed, I'm Trudy Lake. Pleased to meet you!"

It's only a few words, but it takes her a long time to say them. I don't mind. I love southern girls and the way they talk. Used to love them, I mean.

"Trudy Lake?"

"Yes, sir?"

"I'm going to take a wild guess you're not from New York City."

"Oh, Lord, no," she says. "And if I knew the ball team here was called Yankees, I probably would've said no to livin' here."

I laugh. "Where are you from?"

"You know Ralston, Kentucky?"

"Nope."

"Dead Horse Holler?"

"Nope."

"Tate's Crick?"

"Are you from any of those places?"

"No sir. I was just tryin' to zero you in. Let's just say I'm a western Kentucky girl, and leave it at that."

"That'll work. Are you the housekeeper?"

"I'm the girlfriend."

"Dr. Box has a *girlfriend?* Or do I have the wrong number?"

"Hard to believe, but yeah, he's got a girlfriend. And I'm her."

"Is he there?"

"He sure is. Would you like to speak to him?"

"Not really. Not after talking to you. But I need to."

"Hold on, I'll get him."

When Box gets on the phone he says, "I thought it went well with Kathleen last night, didn't you?"

"No."

"Why not?"

"I just started a relationship with Callie. I thought you knew that."

"I did. But Kathleen wanted to see you, after all those years. She wanted you to meet Addie."

"How is that any of your business?"

"I try to help where I can."

"There's a helluva lot more going on than you realize. With regard to me and Kathleen."

"I only did it because I thought I was helping her."

"Had I not just spoken to Trudy I would've bet money you set up the dinner date so you could make a play for Kathleen. You know, show her what a shit I really am, help her gain closure on our relationship. You'd be perfectly positioned to pick up the pieces afterward, have a chance to slide right into her life."

He pauses. "That's actually very astute. To be honest, that was my original plan, exactly. But days after setting up the dinner date with Kathleen I met Trudy. When we became a couple, I tried to cancel the dinner date, since there was nothing in it for me. But Kathleen put a big guilt trip on me about Addie. Said Addie had her heart set on meeting you, and it wasn't right to take that opportunity away from her."

"That sounds like Kathleen."

"Later on, when I realized you and Callie were a couple, I called Kathleen to cancel. But she said if I didn't go through with it she'd tell the hospital board what I did."

"What did you do?"

"It's a bit embarrassing."

"Spit it out."

He whispers, "After performing the surgical procedure that saved Addie's life I asked Kathleen if she'd reward me with a blow job."

"*What?*"

"I did the surgery for free. She was very grateful. She said she had no idea how she could ever repay me. So I suggested a blow job."

I pull the phone away from my ear and stare at it. Did he really just say that? And did he actually *do* that?

I put the phone back to my ear and say, "Whatever the reason, you could've royally fucked up my life. I had my phone on the whole time. Callie was listening from outside the restaurant."

"Well, that was bad judgment on your part. You can't blame me for that."

"I thought I was being ambushed. She was my backup."

"Oh, please. I wouldn't know how to ambush anyone. Not to mention you paid me a hundred million dollars to perform Callie's surgery. Why on earth would I want to cause you harm?"

"You obviously know nothing about my world, or the people who frequent it."

"Thank God for that."

We're quiet till I say, "How old is Trudy Lake?"

"She'll be 19 on Friday."

"She sounds delightful. Is she half as good-looking as she sounds?"

"She's the sixth most beautiful woman I've ever met."

"Why you?"

"Right place, right time. Lots of luck."

"She sounds like a catch."

"Trust me. She is."

"It'd be a shame if anything ever happened to her."

"A *shame*? It'd be a life tragedy! Wait. Are you saying—"

"Stay out of my personal life, Doc. I won't tell you again."

I hang up.

Joe and I catch a cab across the highway and knock on Jill's hotel door. When Frank Sturgiss lets us in I give him a cold look to let him know what I think about his lack of loyalty. Then I introduce Joe and myself to Jill and the sketch artist and ask to see what he's drawn.

"Nothing," he says. "She refuses to talk."

I look at Jill.

She says, "I'll do the sketch when you kill Bobby."

I tell her Joe and I plan to blow Bobby to hell shortly after midnight.

But that's not good enough for her.

"He's just a kid," she says, looking at Joe. "Do you have any idea how powerful Bobby DiPiese is?"

"Bobby's a pussy," I say.

She looks at Frank, who says, "If Mr. Creed says the kid can kill Bobby, you can go ahead and order the headstone."

I add, "Don't forget I found Jack Tallow."

"Finding him isn't the same as rescuing him."

"It won't be easy getting him out of jail. He killed a guy."

"Can they prove it?"

"I think so. He hung the dead body on the back of a tow truck and drove it through downtown Baton Rouge."

She smiles. "Jack's one of a kind. But if you're planning to spring him from jail there's something else you should know."

"Tell me."

"He killed some deer hunters near Jackson, Mississippi."

"How many, specifically?"

"Four."

"When?"

"Monday night."

"It just gets better and better, doesn't it?"

"The cops probably haven't linked Jack to the deer hunters yet, but they will. So you'd better get your ass in gear if you want your sketch."

"Excuse me?"

"Save Jack or kill Bobby. Your choice. Then you'll get your sketch."

I look at Frank. He clearly has a thing for Jill.

But he knows me.

And he's worried.

As he should be.

He says, "Mr. Creed. Before you say or do anything, can I have a minute to talk to her?"

I wave him off while deciding if I should go ahead and beat the shit out of her and force her to do the sketch. It's a tough call because although she's delaying my investigation, I know her description will be more accurate if she's cooperating. It's hard to focus on features when you're in pain.

"I'll make you a deal," I say. "Tell me the guy's name, and I'll take you to Baton Rouge to spring Jack. Then we'll do the sketch."

"How can I trust you?"

"You've got no choice. But I need to get Jack out of jail before they find out about the deer hunters."

"I've told you my terms," Jill says.

She's a handful. She thinks she's got the upper hand. But she doesn't have shit.

I know it, Frank knows it.

"I won't ask again," I say.

Frank says, "Jill? Tell Mr. Creed what he wants to know. You have no idea how close you are to royally fucking up."

She says, "Will you come with us to Baton Rouge?"

He says, "That's up to Mr. Creed."

I nod.

Jill says, "Fine. I'll give you more than you're asking for, to show good faith. The crop duster's name was Mike. I don't know his last name, but he ran drugs for Bobby. The terrorist's name is Ryan Decker. Bobby hired Decker to blow up Jack's lake house because he knew I was there. After I escaped, Decker decided to spare me, and told Bobby I died in the explosion. Happy?"

"No, but it's a start."

I thank the sketch artist for his time and escort him out. I'll get someone in Baton Rouge to sketch Decker's likeness after I spring Jack from the Baton Rouge jail.

Chapter 10

BATON ROUGE SHERIFF Emo Pike isn't just heavy, he's literally bursting at the seams. He motions me to sit. When I do, he says, "Jack Tallow."

"That's right."

He coughs out one of those wheezing, fat guy laughs and says, "Jack claims he never knew there was half a man's torso hanging from the back of the tow truck he was drivin'."

"That's good enough for me," I say. "Go ahead and release him."

He chuckles. "When the calls started hittin' my office Jack was barrelin' down the interstate at 70 miles an hour. You gotta picture this. The bottom half of a dead man's body is swingin' back and forth, blood and guts flyin' everywhere, but damned if he don't just keep comin', all the way to Baton Rouge. But does he stop at the city limits? Hell no!

He circles the whole damn city and winds up downtown. Take a guess what he does next."

I actually don't know. I thought that was the whole story. So I shrug.

Sheriff Pike says, "Jack drives a half-mile down the center of Government Street, sees an all-night gas station, makes a wide u-turn, pulls up to one of the gas pumps, and stops short. That causes the torso to swing around so hard it crashes into one of the pumps, where it does some minor damage, and somehow gets hopelessly hung up in the top half of the pump. This is the body Jack claims not to have noticed."

Pike chuckles till tears form in the corners of his eyes. Then he says, "The guy workin' the gas station's Pakistani. Tahir Hesbani. It's his first fuckin' night on the job. Been in the USA exactly two days. All his life he's heard how violent Americans are, but always thought that was propoganda.

"Tahir's cousin got him a work visa, found him a job at the gas station. Tahir's been workin' the late shift by himself for all of eight minutes when Jack Tallow pulls into the station with a man's bloody torso swingin' from the back of a tow truck. You could've murdered Tahir's whole family, he wouldn't have screamed any louder. He hits the floor, starts to call 911, but hears someone tappin' on the glass above him. It's Jack, tryin' to pay for his gas in advance. Tahir takes one look at Jack, who's bleedin' from head to toe from wild hog bites, and tells him to take whatever he can. Jack hisses at the guy and scares him half to death. See, he can't talk because his vocal cords have been cut out. So he motions for a pen and paper. Tahir supplies it, and Jack writes that Tahir has to unlock the pump. Well, to do that, Tahir has to stand up. So he does, and realizes he's dumped four pounds of shit in his drawers! He unlocks the gas pump and watches Jack fill the truck. But he won't call the cops 'cause he thinks everything that happens in America winds up on the Internet and he doesn't want the whole world to know he shit his pants."

"Makes sense," I say.

"But Jack won't leave. After fillin' the tank he comes back to ask directions. Want to guess what he's lookin' for?"

"A doctor?"

"A veterinarian. To patch up his hog bites. Then he asks Tahir what nationality he is. When he says Pakistani, Jack asks, 'Where can I find a rocket launcher?'"

He laughs. "Bear in mind, all these questions are bein' written down on paper, which means they're evidence! So Jack walks back to the truck, starts it up, puts it in gear, all while forgettin' the dead body's organs are hung up in the broken glass of one of the pumps. He winds up pullin' the top half of the gas pump behind him, and of course, it's scrapin' the ground, makin' a God-awful sound. Later, Jack insists he had no clue there was a body hangin' from the tow truck! He drives about 20 yards before he's surrounded by a dozen squad cars and Baton Rouge Swat. They put him face down on the street and ask what the fuck he's doin' with a body hangin' from the hoist, and you know what he says?"

"Tell me."

"He says the cops must have put it there while he was on the ground. You know, like they were plantin' evidence, like it was some kind of fuckin' dime bag!"

I say, "I believe him. Let him go."

"Good one."

"It's not a joke. I've come here to get him. You'll have to turn him over."

"Like hell I will! We traced the truck to Bobby DiPiese. Ever heard of him?"

"I have."

"We figure Jack is one of Bobby's goons, though he claims he never heard of Bobby, and has no idea who was hangin' from the truck."

"I believe him," I say. "Open his cell. I'll take it from here."

"You're insane."

"The guy's a good Samaritan. A hero."

"*What?*"

"He found the truck at night. Hurt as he was, he attempted to drive it all the way to your police station. He was even willing to fill the gas tank for the owner."

"Uh huh. And the body?"

"It was dark when he found the truck. He didn't see the torso hanging from the hook."

"Bullshit! He pumped gas in a station lit up like Rockerfeller Square! Oh, and the pump he used was five feet from the one he intended to use because, as I said, the body was hung up on the gas pump next to his truck!"

"He was hog bit, right?"

"So?"

"He was probably delirious by the time he made it to the gas station."

"In which case he shouldn't have been drivin'."

"I agree. Charge him for reckless endangerment and release him to my custody."

"You're as crazy as he is."

I press a button on my cell phone, explain the situation to the White House. They contact the U.S. Attorney General's office, and thirty minutes later, Jack's in my limo, reunited with Jill. You'd think she'd be all over him, but when he tries to embrace her she pushes him away, wrinkles her nose, and says, "The stink coming off you makes pig shit smell like honeysuckle."

As we wait for the sketch artist to show up my thoughts turn to Callie. I wonder what she had planned in New York City that was so important she had to get back right away.

Chapter 11

Callie and Kathleen.

CALLIE'S ALONE IN Kathleen's living room, peeking through the blinds. Here's what she knows: Addie has band practice till 5:30, and Kathleen should already be home, since she gets off work at 3:05.

Must be nice being a teacher, she thinks. Home by 3:30, weekends off, winter breaks, Thanksgiving, two weeks for Christmas, twelve weeks' summer vacation....

Callie's eyes are drawn to a chubby girl with pink hair walking on the sidewalk in front of Kathleen's house. As she passes by, Callie notices a printed message on the butt of her sweatpants that reads, "What Would Scooby Doo?"

Seems like everyone's got something written on their asses these days.

Kathleen's car suddenly turns the corner, pulls into the driveway. When Kathleen enters the house she goes straight to the bathroom. Callie gives her a moment of privacy, while listening at the door. The toilet flushes, then Kathleen washes her hands. She opens the door, sees Callie and screams.

"What the hell are you doing in my home?" she shouts.

"You know who I am?"

Kathleen regains her composure. "Of course. I saw you at Donovan's fake funeral, remember? But never mind that. I don't want you here. Please leave, before I call the police."

Callie laughs. "That has to be the emptiest threat I've ever heard. I could kill you before you take two steps toward the phone."

"What do you want?"

"Shall I get straight to the point?"

"Please do."

"No small talk? No polite chatter?"

"Wrong woman, wrong place. What do you want?"

"Offer me some tea."

"Fuck you."

Callie says, "There she is. The real Kathleen. Thanks for letting her out. That makes it so much easier for me."

Kathleen says nothing, just glares at her, seething with fury.

Callie says, "Let's sit in the living room."

"I don't think so."

"I insist."

"I have to pick Addie up from band practice."

"In an hour. Now come, sit. I have a question for you. It's about Addie."

Kathleen follows her into the living room, sits on the couch. Callie chooses the straight-backed chair directly opposite.

Kathleen says, "What could you possibly want to ask me about my daughter?"

"I was wondering what arrangements you've made for her."

"What are you talking about?"

"Arrangements. You know, for Addie's future. In the event something happens to you."

"Are you *threatening* me?"

"Not yet."

Kathleen frowns. "I don't have much practice conversing with murderers. Perhaps you should just say what's on your mind."

"Very well. I'd like to ask about your intentions."

"My...*what? Intentions?*"

"That's right."

"With regard to...?"

"Donovan Creed."

"Oh. Well, that's *my* business, isn't it?"

Callie studies Kathleen's posture. This woman clearly has no idea how to defend herself. She's leaning back on the couch, neck and head behind her torso, which means Callie could deliver a death strike faster than Kathleen could shift her body forward.

"Stay away from Creed," Callie says. "I won't ask again."

"That was asking?"

"Call him, text him, contact him in any way, for any reason..."

"And?"

"I'll kill you with less concern than I'd show a stink bug."

"You're a real charmer. I can see why Donovan's so crazy about you."

"Consider this your last warning."

Kathleen smiles. "You don't have the ability to frighten me...Bitch!"

Callie's right eyebrow arches the slightest bit. Other than that, there's no change in her expression. She looks at the frumpy creature on the couch and wonders what Creed could have possibly seen in her.

And what was it she just said? That I don't have the ability to frighten her?

Creed always says there are two ways to fight someone: your way and his. And your way is better. I agree.

Callie's eyes go vacant. Her voice goes flat. "Think again, Kathleen. Because when you're gone, I'll have Creed manipulate the system."

"What's that supposed to mean?"

"He and I will gain full custody of Addie, regardless of your wishes. And guess who'll spend the most time with her? Me. I'll teach her everything I know about guns, poisons, and fighting. I'll introduce her to my world, and teach her to kill."

"That is utter bullshit. Donovan would never allow it."

"No? Ask me what *his* daughter's doing for a living these days."

"Kimberly?"

"She's in the business now. Except that she goes by the code name Maybe Taylor."

Kathleen's eyes go wide.

Callie says, "Don't fuck with me, Kathleen. Because I not only *will* kill you, I *want* to. Now give me your cell phone."

Kathleen's face goes red. "What do you mean?"

"You've been recording this entire discussion."

Kathleen pauses, then produces her cell phone. Callie clicks rewind, and listens to their conversation.

"I should kill you now and get it over with."

"I won't call Donovan. You have my word."

Callie erases the recording, then gives her a long, hard look. "And if he contacts you?"

"I'll tell him to never call again."

Callie says, "I know what you're thinking. You should have left well enough alone. You shouldn't have met him for dinner. That's right, you shouldn't have. But you did. And now you've got me in your life and I bet you wish there was something you could do to make me go away."

"Yes."

"Not going to happen. It's a near certainty that the last face you'll see on this earth before dying is mine. Because we can't trust each other. It might eventually cross your mind to run away, quit your job, change your identity, try to find a safe place to raise Addie. But deep down you know that won't work because you know what I'm capable of."

"Yes."

"Except you don't."

"Excuse me?"

"You have no idea what I'm capable of."

Callie reaches into her handbag, removes a folded sheet of paper, hands it to Kathleen.

She reads it silently, then says, "Addie's school would never allow you to pick her up. Not in a million years. Especially after I warn them."

"But you signed it, yes?"

Kathleen studies the signature. "How did you do that?"

"Think about what I can do with your signature. Your last will and testament? Addie's inheritance? By this time tomorrow I'll own your identity, which means I can destroy your credit in a matter of minutes. Sell your house without your knowledge. Clean out your bank accounts. Read your emails. Monitor your phone calls and activities. Take over your social media accounts. Send letters to your friends and colleagues that will convince them you're bi-polar. Destroy every romantic relationship you attempt to have. Make Addie a social pariah by frightening the parents of her friends. Is any of this sinking in?"

Kathleen starts to speak, changes her mind.

"Say it," Callie says.

"You're evil. Pure evil."

"Not true. If I were pure evil I'd kill Addie to prove I'm serious." She pauses. "But I would never punish her for something you did." She pauses again. "Unless I had to."

Kathleen says, "You won't have to."

Callie tosses Kathleen's cell phone back to her and says, "Call him."

"Excuse me?"

"Call Creed. On speaker. Tell him it was nice to see him last night, but make sure he knows it's over. You want no contact. You can't be friends. Be convincing."

"I don't have his number."

"That's a lie." Callie says. Then adds, "I didn't realize you were a liar."

"I'm not a liar. I simply forgot."

"That's the first thing a liar would say."

Kathleen has a different concern in mind, and voices it. "When I call Donovan? What if he says he wants to see me?"

Callie says, "That would be really bad. For both of you."

She removes a handgun from her bag and attaches a silencer to it. Then points it at Kathleen's face and says, "Call him. Let's see what he has to say."

Chapter 12

CREED ANSWERS THE phone by saying, "Not a good idea, Kathleen."

"I agree. That's why I'm calling. I wanted to be clear."

"Go ahead."

"Last night was fun. And good for Addie, I think. But I didn't want you to get the wrong impression."

"What's the right impression?"

"I have no interest in reconnecting. It's not you, it's your lifestyle."

"I feel the same way. But I thought I made that clear last night, before leaving."

"You did. But there's one thing we left unsaid."

"What's that?"

"I'd prefer you never call me again, or contact me in any way."

He pauses. "That seems like an odd request. I already told you Callie and I are a couple. Why would I call or contact you?"

"You shouldn't."

Callie motions her to hang up.

Kathleen says, "What I'm trying to say, I don't want to contact you again, and hope you understand. We're different people now."

"Okay. Strange conversation, since we already had it last night, but thanks for making it even more clear. I'll lose your number and you'll lose mine."

"Thank you, Donovan."

"I wish you and Addie all the best."

"You, too."

They hang up and Callie says, "Where do you keep your dildo?"

"My *what?*"

"Dildo."

"I don't have one of those."

"Are you lying again?"

Kathleen squeezes her eyes shut, shakes her head slightly. Then says, "There might be something on the top shelf of my bedroom closet."

"Get it."

Kathleen's eyes go wide. "You wouldn't *dare!*"

Callie says, "Don't flatter yourself."

She follows Kathleen to the bedroom closet, waits for her to produce the dildo. When she does, Callie says, "Pretend that's Creed. And show me what he likes."

"*What?*"

"You're drab. Unkempt. Mousy."

"I—*What?*"

"Your makeup's a mess, your wardrobe sucks, you're barely fit, your tits are small, you slouch when you sit, and you walk like you're pushing a grocery cart....And yet you managed to keep Creed interested enough to consider marriage."

"I can see how that would be hard for you to fathom."

"I've been through your refrigerator and cupboard."

"Excuse me?"

"You can't cook."

"Does that mean you won't be joining us for dinner? Darn!"

"You're unfunny, unexciting, colorless, and have a child. There's only one possible explanation I can come up with for the attraction."

"What's that?"

"You must have been really good in bed."

"I'm not comfortable discussing that part of our relationship with you."

"Would you be more comfortable if I cut off your ears?"

Kathleen looks at the switchblade in Callie's hand and wonders how it got there. Her hand was empty, now it's holding a switchblade, but no time passed between the two events. She says, "You can't be serious about this. I mean, sex is sex. We didn't do anything weird, adventurous, or special."

Callie's not pleased with the response.

Not pleased at all.

"Before I leave, you'll tell me everything you did to him sexually, and everything he did to you. You'll give me details. Favorite position. Favorite place. Did he tie you up? Did he pull your hair? Did you slap each other? Did he spank you? Did you role play? You're going to tell me what he liked, what he responded to, and how you reacted to everything he did."

"I have no idea what that last part means."

"It means you're going to describe every sound you made while having sex. Every whimper and moan. If you cried softly in your pillow or yelled "Oh God!" at the top of your lungs, I want to hear about it. Then you're going to demonstrate."

"How?"

"By using the dildo and pretending its Creed."

"You're insane."

"I'm thorough. Consider it prep."

"For what?"

"Not that I owe you an answer, but I intend to be the best lover Creed's ever had. And if you try to throw in something that never happened, I'll eventually find out. And when I do, I'll make you pay for it."

"How could you possibly find out?"

"I'll ask him."

"He'd never tell."

Callie smiles. "He'll tell me anything I want to know, because I know how to ask him."

"Then why don't you? Why don't you just ask him about the things we did?"

"That's too direct. We'll role play. I'll tell him to pretend I'm you. Then I'll start doing all the things you did to him, exactly the way you did them. I'll walk him through it. At some point he'll either say, "Yes!" or he'll say, "No, Kathleen would never have done that." And if he says that—"

Kathleen thinks about it. "You're holding a knife."

"That's right."

"You're not going to make me take off my clothes, are you?"

"That depends."

"On what?"

"The kiss."

"What kiss?"

"I don't care to see you naked, and shouldn't have to if you give me a proper explanation of how you had sex. But you won't be able to explain how you kissed him. That's something you'll have to demonstrate."

"How?"

"By kissing me, and pretending I'm Creed."

"That's ridiculous! I could never do that."

"You'll be amazed what you can do if I insist. And I will."

"But...you're gay."

"You're just saying that because my sexual history has been influenced by gender confusion. But don't think for a minute I'll enjoy kissing you, because I'd rather lick the scab off a dead dog's foreskin."

Kathleen winces with disgust.

Callie says, "Kissing you is research. Nothing else."

"How long is this going to take?"

"That's up to you."

They kiss. Tentatively, at first, but after a few minutes Kathleen gets caught up in it. By the time Callie's satisfied with the experiment, Kathleen's face and neck are flushed.

"Lie on the bed and show me your moves," Callie says.

A very mortified Kathleen demonstrates the various positions and tries to convey the pillow talk as best she can, but it's coming across like a third-grader's current events report.

"I'm not impressed," Callie says.

Kathleen shrugs.

They go back to Kathleen's den and sit. Callie pulls her phone from her jeans' pocket and presses the notebook app.

"What now?" Kathleen says.

"Q and A."

"You're joking."

"Question number one. Tell me about the first time you had sex with Creed. Leave nothing out."

Kathleen shakes her head. "It doesn't work that way."

"What doesn't?"

"You can't just clinically analyze the magic that occurred between two people and try to reproduce it."

"How do you know? Have you ever tried?"

"No, of course not. But you should just be yourself."

"Being yourself is another way of saying you didn't bother to prepare."

"What do you mean?"

"This is the big difference between you and me, Kathleen. It's why I'm better for him than you. Creed is easy to catch, but hard to keep. Somehow—don't ask me how—you managed to catch him. But you blew it. You tried to keep him by just being yourself. Creed is a goal to achieve. A mountain to scale. A prize to not only win but hold on to. I'm willing to put in the time and effort necessary to give him the best *me* I can be. But to do that, I need to know everything about him."

"And if you learn things you don't like?"

"I'll uncover them during the discovery phase, and practice dealing with them in advance. Consider it due diligence."

"*Discovery* phase? Due *diligence*? This is how you define the romantic part of your relationship?"

"How about I ask the questions and you answer them."

"How many are there?"

Callie consults her list. "One hundred forty-three."

Kathleen frowns. "You know I have to pick Addie up in a few minutes."

"Fine. We'll pick her up together."

"That's not going to happen."

"Then get someone else to pick her up."

Kathleen sighs. "If I answer all your questions, and promise never to contact Donovan, will you leave me alone and never bother me again?"

"If and if? Yes."

"I'll call and have one of the moms pick Addie up from band practice. But let's move this along as quickly as possible."

Kathleen makes the call, then says, "What's the second question on your list?"

Callie says, "Spit or swallow?"

Kathleen winces. "For the love of God, Callie."

"I'm waiting."

"Spit. What's question three?"

"What's his preference, mouth or hand? And why? And how long does it usually take? Oh, and I guess you'll need to get the dildo again, because I'll require demonstrations."

Kathleen shakes her head as if trying to wake up from a bad dream. "Just out of curiosity, what's the last question?"

"It's a long one."

"Let's hear it."

"Did you give him anal? If so, how many times? If so, did he ask for it, or just do it? If he asked, how did he phrase the question? Did you comply? If not, how did you turn him down? And if you did, why? And if you did, how did he react?"

Kathleen closes her eyes, shakes her head. "You can't be serious."

"You know I am."

The question and answer portion of the discovery phase lasts nearly two hours. When it finally comes to an end, Callie says, "So basically, if you're to be believed, you did every single thing that could be done sexually."

"Not everything. If I remember correctly, question 38 involved threesomes, couple-swapping, and participating in orgies. I never did any of that."

Callie consults her notes. "According to you, he never asked. So your non-participation's a technicality, isn't it."

She stands, walks toward the front door.

Kathleen says, "My opinion? This relationship isn't going to work out."

Callie says, "My opinion? You're a slut!"

Chapter 13

Ryan Decker.

"THERE'S ONE WAY in and one way out," Decker says. "This road goes 70 yards and turns into Goodman Circle, an exclusive neighborhood with eight magnificent homes. And yes, it's an actual circle."

Decker and his three lieutenants are standing near the entrance to Goodman Circle, in Brookfield, Kentucky. They're dressed in work uniforms with matching helmets.

"I thought it'd be more secluded," Martin says.

"It's actually quite secluded, considering it's less than a quarter-mile from the interstate that divides Brookfield from Louisville's East End."

"How big are the lots?"

"Five acres each. And the circle's surrounded by woods and a golf course. If we park the semi here, we can isolate the entire neighborhood."

"We'll need two semis for the motorcycles, equipment, and manpower."

"Noted."

One of the other men, Corrigan, says, "What are these houses worth?"

"Two to six million."

"They'll have alarms."

"That's a good thing."

"Why?"

"Two reasons. First, it'll force us to strike with speed and precision. Second, we'll generate maximum publicity."

"Why?"

"When you frighten the rich, you terrify the poor and middle class."

Burroughs says, "It's a perfect target. But a big step for us."

"For you, yes. But I blew up half of Leeds Road in Willow Lake, Arkansas, last night. That was a logistical nightmare. This mission's a snap compared to that one."

An elderly resident slows to a stop and asks, "Is everything all right?"

"Yes, ma'am," Decker says. "We're just finishing up."

She points at his helmet. "What does BWC stand for?"

"Brookfield Water Company."

"There's not a problem with our water, is there?"

"No ma'am. This area has the highest-quality, best-tasting water in the entire country, thanks to dedicated field men like these," he says, indicating his lieutenants.

"Well, keep up the good work, then," she says.

"Will do. Have a nice day."

When she drives off Martin says, "Nice lady. Think she'll survive?"

"We'll know soon enough."

Chapter 14

Milo Fister, Faith Stallone, Maybe Taylor.

MILO'S PHONE RINGS. "It's her. Let's go."

Faith says, "I can't believe we're meeting a contract killer in your parking lot in the middle of the morning."

"Her first choice was a secluded rest stop in the middle of the night. Which do *you* think is safer?"

"Neither."

Milo's office is on the eighth floor of what locals call *The Flashcube Building*, which is the centerpiece of a large suburban Louisville office complex. He and Faith climb in their respective cars and drive to the farthest corner of the parking lot, where they park, leaving an empty space between their cars, as directed.

Milo gets out of his car and approaches Faith's Mercedes.

She lowers the window.

He says, "What if she asks us to get in her car?"

"We'll say no. What's she going to do, shoot us in the parking lot? In broad daylight? What're we, fifty yards from Shelbyville Road? Nonstop traffic? She'd never chance it."

"Okay. Let's make a pact. We don't get in her car under any circumstances."

"I thought I just made that clear, Milo."

"You did. I'm just thinking out loud. I do that whenever I'm about to meet a stone killer face to face."

"You think she's already killed Byron Zass?"

"No. She said she'd give us proof."

"His dead body in the trunk would be proof."

"She'd have to prove he's dead. Not passed out, or drugged."

"And what medical background do we possess that would help us make that determination?"

"None. Which is why she'll need to prove it, somehow."

Faith says, "What made you choose Byron? You just met him once, at dinner."

"That's the first reason. I don't know him. But the second is, he's dating Lexi, right in front of her husband."

"Ex-husband."

"They're separated, not divorced."

"A technicality."

"Maybe so. But it's way too soon to bring him into the group. You saw how it affected Brody. I half expected him to slit his wrists in his car after dinner."

"Killing Byron won't make her go back to Brody."

"Probably not. But it'll make Brody feel better to know Lexi lost someone that was important to her."

"You're being awfully hard on Lexi. She may have stopped loving Brody, but at least she never cheated on him. That's more than I can say for your wife and my husband."

"Did you see the way Zass smirked at Brody when I said she was faithful? I guarantee you they were having an affair before she and Brody separated. By the way, we're both supposed to be out of our cars, standing in front of your hood. And our hands have to be empty."

"Whatever."

Seconds after Milo and Faith get in position, a nondescript black sedan starts moving slowly toward them, and parks in the vacant space between their cars. A young woman gets out.

"That can't be her," Faith whispers. "She's a child."

Milo shrugs.

The girl says, "Call me Maybe."

"Like the song?" Faith says.

"I came up with that name *months* before the song came out," Maybe says, indignantly.

"I don't know," Faith says. "That would be a big coincidence."

"Faith?" Milo says, with a warning tone.

She ignores him. "If I were you," Faith says, "I'd change it."

"Maybe I'll change it to Lexi," she says.

Milo and Faith exchange a look.

Before Milo can say, "Why Lexi?" Maybe says, "Come closer, but don't scream."

They do, and Maybe pops open the trunk.

There's no reason to scream.

Nothing to see but plastic tarpaulin, which is everywhere. There's so much tarp it's bulging out of the trunk. Maybe grabs a corner piece and lifts it high enough for them to see Lexi's face.

Lexi's face?

Lexi's. And she's clearly not alive.

Milo and Faith don't need proof. What they need is an explanation.

After looking around to see if anyone's watching, Milo says, "I told you Byron Zass. Not Lexi Lynch."

Maybe motions them to the other side of the trunk, lifts up another section of tarp.

"You asked, I delivered. Say hi to Byron."

Byron's past communicating. And again, Milo and Faith don't bother to ask for proof. The fact that Byron is dead would be obvious to even the most casual observer. Nevertheless, Maybe says, "In case it crossed your mind he might be asleep, drugged, or playing possum, I will now demonstrate he's 100% dead."

She fishes a butane lighter from the trunk, clicks the flame on, and says, "Milo, run your finger over the flame to verify it's hot."

"I-I don't require proof, Ms. Taylor."

"I insist."

Milo puts his hand above the flame a second, then pulls it away. "It's quite hot."

"Faith? Your turn."

She puts her hand over the flame and confirms it's hot.

Maybe says, "This is an authentic butane lighter. Not methane, or propane, which top out around—I'm going to give you round numbers here—2,700 and 3,000 degrees, respectively. Butane will hit temperatures as high as 3,600 degrees. Not that it matters much, since human flesh starts to burn at 140 degrees."

She puts the flame to Byron's cheek and roasts it for fifteen seconds, creating a plume of smoke with a vile stench.

She says, "If he were playing possum, he'd have twitched by now, don't you think?"

Milo and Faith are unable to respond, since opening their mouths would be enough to induce vomiting. While Faith's gagging, her eyes are rimmed with tears. "I can't believe you killed Lexi. She was our friend."

Maybe says, "Burning flesh smells a bit like pork in a frying pan, but the outer skin has a rancid odor, don't you think?"

"Please stop!" Faith says, through gritted teeth. Both she and Milo have turned away. They're covering their noses with their right hands.

"You're convinced he and Lexi are dead?" Maybe says.

"I can't speak for Faith," Milo says, "but I was convinced the moment I saw there were no bodies attached to the heads."

"Well, I didn't want there to be any doubt. Hold out your hands."

They do, and Maybe drops two objects into each of their hands.

"What's this?" Milo says.

"Souvenirs. Lexi's nipples for you, Byron's testicles for Faith."

Faith retches, and allows her souvenirs to fall to the ground. Milo inspects Lexi's nipples, then sniffs them. The look of disgust he receives from Faith is worse than the one she gave Byron's testicals.

Maybe closes the trunk and says, "You're going to need iron-clad alibis. It's best if you're both out of town on the same night. In different cities."

Faith says, "Assuming we give you the go-ahead, when would it happen?"

"Whoa," Maybe says. "*Assuming* you give me the go-ahead?" She laughs. "The go-ahead for killing your spouses is in the trunk of this rental car. There's no turning back. You're in now, both of you. You can change your mind about Jake and Lemon, but you're going to pay me whether I kill them or not."

"We understand," Milo says. "When will it take place?"

"What works best for you guys?" Maybe says, as casually as if planning a dinner date.

They look at each other. "We'll get back to you," Faith says.

"No. You'll decide right now, by the time I get back."

"Where are you going?" Milo says.

She points to the hardware store on the other side of the parking lot and says, "I need to make a copy of your house keys."

"I don't think so," Faith says.

"Think again."

Milo says, "I thought you'd be able to pick the locks."

"It's a lot easier to use a key."

"But if you're staging a home invasion, wouldn't you break the door down?"

"*Afterward*, Milo. You stage the crime scene *after* killing the marks."

"Why?"

"Because you can't know exactly what will happen before going in. When they're dead, and everything's set up exactly the way I want, I'll walk out, lock the door, kick it in, run away. Doesn't that sound easier?"

"Makes sense," Milo says.

"If you're going to kill them in Milo's house you shouldn't need *my* key," Faith says.

"We don't know whose house they'll be in that night. They might go to a hotel, for that matter. You're paying me to do a job. To do it right I need to be prepared."

"I understand that. It's just—"

"I can pick your lock, Faith. I'd just prefer not to. Do you really want to piss me off over a fucking house key?"

Faith frowns, produces her key ring, removes her house key, places it in Maybe's palm. Milo does the same.

"I'll be right back," she says.

Ten minutes later she says, "What have you worked out?"

"How do we pay you?" Milo says.

"Glad you asked. She fetches two small canvass bags from her back seat, hands them over. "You'll start assembling the cash immediately. Every few days you'll cash checks for various amounts. No single check can be more than $9,900, but they have to total at least $20,000 a week, every week, till I'm paid in full. You'll collect the money in these bags and place them in your attics every Sunday night. I may pick them up every week, or let them accumulate. I might not pick them up for a year. Don't worry about that part. Just do your part."

"How will you get in our attics?" Faith says.

"Don't worry about that part. Just make sure you keep putting the cash in the bags every Sunday night before going to bed. And don't make the mistake of trying to fuck me over."

"Week after next," Milo says. "I'm playing in a weekend golf tournament in South Carolina. I'll be leaving Friday morning."

"Friday the 13th? I like it. Start gathering your cash today."

"What about me?" Faith says.

"Call your sister, the one who lives in Denver."

Faith's expression shows she's not happy a killer knows where her sister lives.

Maybe says, "Tell her you're coming to see her on the 13th. You'd like to stay a couple nights. "She'll say yes, don't you think?"

Faith nods.

"Send an email to follow up on the conversation. Buy a couple of presents for her kids today, and wrap them. The trip and presents will be on record. If you're both out of town it's highly likely Jake and Lemon will get together that night, don't you think?"

"It's a certainty," Faith says.

"If they hook up, I'll kill them together. If not, I'll kill them individually. It'll either be a home invasion or a murder-suicide."

"What's the motivation for that?"

"Someone will know about the affair. It can't be you guys, but trust me, someone will know. When the cops find out, the pieces will fall into place. You might be suspects, but your alibis are excellent. And they won't find out about me unless you tell them. And that would be a mistake." She pauses a minute, picks Byron's nuts off the pavement, puts them in her jeans pocket. Then says, "Any questions?"

Faith and Milo look at each other.

No, they don't have any questions.

Chapter 15

Donovan Creed, Joe Penny,
Jack & Jill.

JACK TALLOW LOOKS like shit. He's juiced up with pain
meds and antibiotics and writing stories about Jill's husband
that are impossible to believe.

Writing them on a yellow legal pad, since he can't
speak.

Bobby Dee had a doctor remove his vocal cords so he
wouldn't make too much noise while being tortured. But he
didn't have time to be tortured too badly in the basement
because Bobby had his goons dump Jack in a pen full of wild
hogs near the Blood River. From what I've pieced together,
Jack's escape involved killing two guys and stealing a truck.
But the details are sketchy, and I'm not interested enough to
question him further.

If Jack's to be believed, Bobby has a number of prisoners chained up in the basement of his antebellum home in La Pierre, Louisiana. And now he's insisting I spare the prisoners.

"I don't give a rat's ass about the prisoners," I say. "And if they look as bad as you, I expect they'll welcome a swift death."

Jack writes:

> *Some of them are kids! The prisoners are part of the state's witness protection program. Bobby sells the snitches to the mob and rapes and tortures the family members.*

"I can see why you didn't get along," I say. "He sounds like a shitty host."

> *You have to save them. You can't just blow them up.*

I look at Joe Penny. "I want this done tonight. Any way to keep the prisoners alive while blowing up the rest of the house?"

"I haven't seen the house, but if it's as big as Jill says, the prisoners have three ways to die and only one way to live."

"Elaborate."

"They could die in the initial blast, be crushed by the rubble, or suffocate from the dust."

"And their chance for living?"

"Pure luck."

"Give me odds."

He looks at Jack. "Are any of them chained to the corners of the basement?"

Jack shakes his head, no.

Joe says, "Then the odds are pretty much zero."

I nod. "Sorry Jack. I've got a country to save."

Jill says, "That's not good enough. I won't have innocent deaths on my conscience."

She looks at Frank and says, "You need to talk to him."

I hold up my hand. "Save your breath, Frank. Jill, I'll remind you the only reason I'm killing Bobby is because that was part of our deal."

"Well, saving the prisoners is our new deal."

Frank shuts his eyes. He doesn't believe the shit that comes out of Jill's mouth any more than I do.

Joe Penny's sitting closer to the limo driver than me, so I say, "Tell our driver to make a circle around the block and ignore whatever happens. And ask him to raise the privacy panel."

Joe tells him what I said.

When the panel's up and the car's moving, I say, "Jill, look at me. I don't *have* to kill your husband. I'm perfectly willing to *force* your cooperation."

Jack starts to puff up like he's going to get physical, but his intentions are interrupted by a wheezing attack.

"You're bleeding," I say, pointing at his thigh.

Jill says, "I won't cooperate if you allow the prisoners to die." She gives me a look of defiance. "Hit me all you want, but it won't make me change my mind."

My first strike crushes Frank's Adam's apple. I had intended to simply slap Jill's face hard enough to show her I'm serious about saving my country, but Frank saw it coming and started to make a move. He's a good man, extremely capable with his fists, so I couldn't afford to let him follow through with his attack. I don't know how Jill flipped him against me so quickly, but like I say, he's a tough guy, and a big one, as well. He shakes off the pain and swings for the fences, but as he does, I've got my hand against his chest, pushing him back, so his punch falls short of the mark. I come back at him with a palm strike that shatters his nose.

There's nothing I hate more than losing a good man, so I apologize to Frank and say, "I hope she at least let you fuck her."

He tries to mount another attack and I hit him as flush and hard as I ever hit a man, and I can practically hear the blood filling his brain pan.

Jill's scream pierces my ears.

She didn't wait till Frank was dying to scream, it's just that Frank was dying before she had time to get the scream out. I go ahead and give Jill the hard slap she earned earlier. While her head goes flying backward, I backhand Jack, who stopped coughing long enough to attempt an assault of his own. I watch Jill's head slam against the wall of the limo and wonder how she feels about that.

Turns out she feels woozy.

Her head caroms off the window and nearly falls into Joe Penny's lap.

I survey the situation. Joe's horrified, Frank's dying, Jack's out cold, and Jill's trying to scratch my eyes out.

I sigh.

Who the hell *are* these people?

When under attack, I have the ability to see things in slow motion. Jill's tougher than I expected. She's coming at me with both hands, trying to slash my face. If she gets close enough she'll try to bite me. I consider grabbing both her hands and crushing them, but as I think on it, a part of me respects her for caring so much about the prisoners in Bobby's basement, so I decide to let her retain the use of her hands. At least for now.

I know what you're thinking.

I'm going soft, right?

I slap Jill's hands away and catch her in the temple with my fist, taking enough off the punch to keep from killing her, while keeping enough in it to knock her out for a full minute.

Frank's dying slowly, suffering.

I hate that.

This would be the perfect time to smash his nose bone into his brain and kill him instantly, like the martial arts guys do in the movies. But I can't do that, because it's a complete myth. The nose isn't made of bone, it's cartilage. And even if it were bone, it wouldn't be strong enough, or long enough, or sharp enough, to penetrate the skull and enter the brain.

Frank's dying from internal hemorrhaging. If we went to a hospital immediately we could save his life and possibly prevent permanent brain damage. But that's out of the question. I can't allow a dangerous guy like Frank to live after he's turned on me. I give him another hard smack on the temple, but my heart's not in it.

By the time Jill regains consciousness, we've circled the block and parked again, and I've secured her wrists and ankles with plastic zip ties.

It takes her a moment to focus, and when she does she yells, "Frank!"

"Don't think for a moment I won't kill you," I say.

She screams.

Jack wakes up. He'd come at me if he could, but I've secured his wrists and ankles, too.

Jill screams a second time, so I try Callie's move of squeezing her throat with my thumb and forefinger to squelch it.

That doesn't work, so I slap her again.

I think about how easily Callie stifled Abbey's scream in the tent this morning. But all I managed to do was piss Jill off. Maybe it's technique. Or maybe my hands are too big.

Now she's crying, and I think I liked her better when she was screaming.

I watch her with interest, and come to the conclusion Sheriff Cox was right: Jill's a fine looking woman. I'd peg her age at 30, and give her face and body a nine. The crying adds an air of vulnerability she probably doesn't deserve, based on how she's treated Jack since he got out of jail. But she's got something going for her. Remember, this is a woman who got Jack's house, money, and credit cards, and turned Frank against me in a matter of minutes.

Her clothes are a mess, but I can overlook that. I like the way her jeans cling to her legs. At the moment, her legs are splayed, the view enticing. Picture Callie's leggings from earlier today, except that Jill's sitting down which enhances the camel toe. I probably shouldn't stare at her crotch like this. It makes me just as bad as the Willow Lake police force, but what can I say? It's, you know, right *there*.

If I wasn't in love with Callie I'd be all over Jill. I'd try to hit that triangle a time or two.

But you're right. I've gone soft. I can't cheat on Callie.

Not that Jill's offering.

Frank's death, plus the latest slap I gave her seems to have finally made an impression on her attitude. She's still crying, but it's muffled. Jack's hissing at me like a stuttering snake, and hissing at her the same way. I assume he's mad at me and trying to comfort her, but it all sounds the same, and she's not happy with him anyway. In fact, I bet she regrets asking me to save Jack. I'm almost certain she would have run off with Frank.

I get my cell phone out and call the sketch artist and learn she's been waiting at the police station. Then I realize I can't put her in the car with a dead guy, so I cancel her and call my geeks and tell Curly to arrange for a sketch artist to meet me in New Orleans, at the Rose Dumont Hotel. I ask if he and the others have had any luck finding Ryan Decker.

"We've found hundreds of Ryan Deckers," he says. "But that's probably not his real name. We need that police sketch. If it's good enough we can run it through law enforcement, social media, and motor vehicles."

"I'm working on it," I say.

We dump Frank's body outside Carville, in a rice field that's been converted to a crawfish farm. Then we ride past

Bobby Dee's house in La Pierre, so Joe can get a good look at what he'll be blowing up, assuming Jill still wants to go through with the plan.

I say, "We can't guarantee the prisoners will live, so I'll let you make the call. I'm willing to blow Bobby and his men up tonight if you want, or we can forget about it. Either way, you're going to cooperate with the sketch artist when we get to New Orleans."

She and Jack exchange a look.

He nods.

She says, "We want you to kill Bobby."

"Maybe some of the prisoners will get lucky and survive," I say, cheerfully.

My phone rings. It's C.H., the elf, calling me with bad news. After hearing the details I look at Jill and say, "I should have beaten that sketch out of you the moment we met."

"What's wrong?"

"Terrorist attack."

Jill knows I'm on edge. She's frightened. Defensive. Says, "You can't just assume Decker's responsible for every terrorist attack that takes place."

I tell her to shut the fuck up. Then I call Callie.

Chapter 16

"WHAT'S UP?" CALLIE says.

"Please tell me you're not in Central Park."

"I'm not."

"Thank God!"

"Why? What's happened?"

"Decker."

"Who's that?"

"The Willow Lake bomber. Ryan Decker, self-proclaimed urban terrorist."

"Shit. What's he done? If he'd set off a bomb in Central Park, I would've heard it."

"Different strategy this time. About 30 minutes ago, scores of college-age men swarmed a section of Central Park."

"What do you mean, 'swarmed'?"

"They attacked several cops and dozens of citizens. Sprayed some sort of aerosol into their faces to disorient them, and knocked them out. Then they pulled their pants down and wrote BWC on their asses."

"That's *insane*! Was anyone hurt?"

"Not that we've heard."

"Then what's the point?"

"I have no idea."

I give Callie a minute to think on it. While waiting, I look out the window and spot a sign covered in bird shit that says New Orleans: 18 miles. I can't get that damn sketch fast enough.

Callie says, "What's his fascination with asses, do you suppose?"

"Humiliation. If you don't want to physically hurt someone, pulling their pants down in public is about as humiliating as it gets. Especially for a cop."

Callie says, "They're doing it to prove they can."

"I agree. And by including cops, they're sending the message they can do whatever they want whenever they want. For the moment, this is what they want. But later on?"

"I'm trying to picture it."

"Which part?"

"Cops lying on the ground, pants around their ankles, messages written on their asses. This might look like a prank, but it's not."

"The media will treat it like a wilding, and the late-night comics will have a field day, but you're right, this is serious. I've never been more concerned about a threat in my entire life."

"What *is* the threat, exactly?"

"That it could catch on. That BWC could wind up being the rallying cry for street thugs, street gangs, nerds, loner-stoners, and every terrorist wannabe in the country. If Decker's group can humiliate cops in broad daylight they can humiliate anyone. Judges. CEO's. Nuns. If they can penetrate the security of Central Park, every ass in Congress could be penetrated."

"Please tell me that last part was an attempt at political humor."

"It was."

"Well, don't give up your day job."

"Okay. On a serious note, what happened in Central Park was an organized, controlled swarm. You know those flash mobs that suddenly show up and start dancing in public places? This was like that."

"But if they're not hurting anyone, what are they after?"

"They're getting our attention. My attention, to be precise."

"Yours?"

"Police found a small portion of a dime novel today, lying beside one of the victims. It's titled, *Emmett Love: Hero of the Western Plains.*"

"So?"

"You remember Rose? The witchy nurse that helped Doctor Box with your operation?"

"Of course."

"She told me I'm Emmett Love's direct descendent."

"Tell me again who Emmett Love was?"

"Original sheriff of Dodge City. Before Wyatt Earp and all the others."

"Maybe it's a coincidence."

"I don't think so. Attached to the cover was a note addressed to Donovan Creed, Agency Director, Sensory Resources. No signature on the note, just the words: *Because We Can!*"

"This guy Decker must be connected to you somehow. Did they catch any of the college kids who were involved?"

"No. They limited their activity to a specific area of the park, and sprayed everyone in it. Then scattered before anyone regained consciousness."

"Then how does anyone know what happened? I can't imagine the victims could provide this much information."

"It's all over the Internet, Callie. Every victim was photographed and videoed."

"By whom?"

"The flash mob. Wait. I'm getting a call. Can you hang on a sec?"

"Of course. Who's calling?"

"Kathleen. Maybe she saw something."

"Gosh, I hope she wasn't one of the victims," Callie says. "Or Addie."

"Hang on, I'll let you know."

I take Kathleen's call, then click back to Callie, who asks if everything's all right.

"They're fine. She and Addie weren't there. She hasn't heard anything about it."

"What did she want?"

"I don't know, but she's been acting weird as hell today. She called earlier to tell me not to call her again. Yet here she is, calling me. She said she needed to tell me something."

"Any idea what?"

"Nope. Just that it's urgent."

"And you replied?"

I told her I was in the middle of a terrorist attack, and said whatever she wanted to tell me would have to wait till I get back to town."

"You've got a lot on your plate. I'm glad she understood."

"I won't call her back if you don't want me to."

"I don't mind. But I do want it to end."

"I'll make that very clear."

"How about you call her tomorrow night, after you get back, and put her on speaker, so I can hear you end things once and for all."

"No problem."

"Thanks, Donovan. By the way, I keep checking my phone for that police sketch. What's the holdup?"

"I'm working on it."

She pauses. "Should I be worried?"

"About what?"

"Jill Whittaker. Or DiPiese, or whatever she's calling herself today."

"What are you saying, exactly?"

"Is she as pretty as Sheriff Cox said?"

"Don't give her a second thought. Or Kathleen. Or anyone else."

"Okay. I trust you."

We hang up, and I notice the car's not moving. The driver informs me we're 16 miles out of New Orleans, stuck in a major traffic jam. There's been a wreck. We're going to be sitting here a while.

"How long's a while?"

"At least an hour. Both lanes are blocked. There's zero movement. Metro traffic says they've got to clear a semi, but it's on the bridge."

"Fuck!"

"Sorry."

I want that sketch. But I'm stuck here, fuming.

Jill's staring at me, and all I can think is if I hadn't put up with her bullshit I might have been able to avoid this Central Park disaster. I reach over and give her face a hard slap.

And now her gorgeous legs are the last thing on my mind.

Chapter 17

I'M FURIOUS WITH her. But every time Jack looks away, Jill gives me a look that's hard to ignore.

If I didn't know better, I'd swear she's coming on to me.

But I *do* know better. She can't possibly be interested in me. I killed Frank Sturgiss, slapped the shit out of her, and refused to save the prisoners in the basement of her house in La Pierre.

Nevertheless, she says, "Can I talk to you in private?"

Jack spins his head around and starts hissing fit to bust.

"What do you have in mind?"

Jill says, "Can Joe and the driver go for a short walk?"

"What about Jack?"

"I'd like him to stay for the first part."

I tell Joe and the driver to walk a short distance, but keep the car in sight. When they leave, Jill says, "I wasn't sure about you at first. But now I am."

"What do you mean?"

She sighs. "This is a little embarrassing for me, but my life has been going at warp speed, and I'm not sure what's going to happen when we get to New Orleans. What I'm trying to say, I'm into you."

Jack's eyes grow wide. He thrashes about, trying to break free from his bonds. He's furious, hissing louder than Elvis fans at a gay parade.

"Oh, shut up, Jack!" she says. "Do you have any idea how annoying that is?"

She looks at me. "Can you cut me loose?"

I cut her zip ties with my pocket knife. She rubs her wrists and says, "I appreciate what you did to help Jack. He's had a rough time."

Hearing this, Jack quiets down. Jill says, "He lost his voice, his dream house, his money...and judging from the blood on his clothes, he's going to need serious medical care for those hog bites."

I'm not sure where she's going with all this talk about Jack, so I just say, "You're welcome."

She says, "I don't want you to blow up Bobby's house. Can you just kill him?"

"What about his goons?"

"That would be a bonus, if you can do it without killing the prisoners. But if not, the goons will clear out when Bobby's dead. And I'll inherit the house."

Jack seems to like what he's hearing. He nods his head enthusiastically.

I say, "You could live in that house? After what happened in the basement?"

"No, of course not! But I'd like to sell it."

"That's taking a practical view."

She stares at Jack a minute, then turns to me and says, "Jack and I were never a couple."

He starts hissing again, violently.

Jill shakes her head. "I feel like we're ride-sharing with a Komodo Dragon." She pauses a minute. "Where was I?"

"You and Jack were never a couple."

Jack starts kicking his feet. I say, "Apparently he disagrees."

"I've been with exactly two men in my entire life," she says.

"I find that quite hard to believe."

"I can understand why you feel that way. But it's true."

"I assume Bobby's one of them?"

She nods.

"And Jack?"

"Don't be ridiculous. I barely know him."

Jack sputters and makes loud, almost maniacal sounds of protest. He searches desperately for his pencil and paper, finds them, and starts writing as furiously as any man with bound wrists could possibly write. Jill grabs his pencil and breaks it in half. Then throws it through the open partition, into the front seat.

"Enough!" she says. "We saved your life, Jack. Be grateful." She turns to me and says, "I'll cooperate with your sketch artist the minute we get to the hotel. And I'll trust you to keep your promise about killing Bobby whenever it works best for your schedule."

"In return for?"

"Protecting me until you kill him."

"And?"

"A new identity and top-quality medical treatment for Jack."

"And?"

"Our time is limited, so I'm just going to toss something out there."

"Go ahead."

"I'm a looner."

"Which means what, exactly?"

"I have a sexual fetish for balloon play."

"I don't know what that means, but I like the sound of it. Thanks for telling me."

"You're welcome. The other thing is I'm insanely attracted to dangerous, powerful men. By attracted, I mean sexually attracted. Frank told me you're the most dangerous man in the world. It wasn't necessary that you have movie star good looks, but it sure as hell doesn't hurt. What I'm trying to say, I want—*need*—you to make love to me."

Jack starts thrashing about, hissing at the highest decibel possible. It's more of a whirring sound, almost like a jet engine. Jill's right, it's annoying as hell.

"Will you do it?" She says. "Will you make love to me?"

"I'm involved with someone."

"So I heard. Callie. But here's the thing: she'll never have to know."

Before I have a chance to tell her it's totally out of the question, she licks her lips and says, "Donovan?"

"Yeah?"

"I'm sopping wet for you."

I look at Jack. "Time for you to go, partner."

I pull him toward me, open the door, push him out, and motion for Joe to come and get him. Then I close the door and say, "Where were we?"

"We were talking about sex."

"Right. What about it?"

"I want it."

"Right. But I'm with Callie."

"You love her?"

"Absolutely."

"Enough to marry her?"

"Yes."

"Did you have your last fling?"

"What do you mean?"

"You're planning to be with the same woman for the rest of your life. In your case that's what, forty years?"

"Not the way I live."

"Well, however much time you've got, you should have the memory of a last fling."

"I already had a last fling."

"Let me define what I mean. A last fling is not necessarily the last person you slept with."

"It's not?"

"No. It only counts as a last fling if you know in advance she's the last person you'll ever sleep with besides your future wife."

"You're confusing me."

"I'll make it simple. The last woman you slept with. What's her name?"

"The last one I slept with or the last one I cared about?"

"The last one you slept with."

I think a minute. "That was more of a one-night stand."

"Had you already committed to Callie?"

"No."

"That's what I mean: You never fucked a woman knowing she'd be the last except for Callie. But I'd be honored to be your last fling, Donovan. I'd be honored to be the one you'll remember for the rest of your life."

"You make a helluva case, Jill. But the thing is, I love Callie."

"More than you love the United States?"

"What do you mean?"

"If it meant saving the country, would you make love to me?"

"That's a strange angle to take."

"I can help you catch Decker."

"How?"

"Let's not get side-tracked. Let's just say I can deliver Decker. How badly do you want him?"

"Very."

"What if you could keep the woman you love, have your last fling with me, and save the country from a series of terrorist attacks?"

"I have to admit, it sounds awfully innocent when you put it that way."

"I can deliver Decker. That makes it your patriotic duty to make love to me."

"You should sell insurance. Or used cars."

"Why?"

"Never mind. What makes you so sure you can get Decker?"

"He asked me to travel with him. I turned him down, but he said to call him if I ever change my mind. If I call him maybe you can do that triangulation thing with his cell phone, and track him down. Or be waiting nearby when he comes to fetch me."

"I thought you barely knew the guy."

"I barely do. I met him just before the explosion. Afterward, he gave me a ride to Memphis."

"That's it?"

She nods.

Throughout the day I've been piecing together information on Jill, Jack, Bobby, and Decker. This seems like a good time to summarize. "Let me see if I've got this right. Your husband, the mob boss, hated losing you so much he hired Decker, the terrorist, to blow up a house in order to kill you."

"That's right."

"Before that, he hired Jack, the bounty hunter, to find you and bring you back."

She nods.

"Jack found you in Kentucky, kidnapped you, and fell hopelessly in love with you during the ride to Louisiana."

She shrugs.

"Jack gave you his money, his house, and asked you to marry him."

"Yup."

"Hours after meeting you."

She nods.

"Darryl Rhodes tried to sexually molest you, and Decker shot him. A few hours later, Decker tried to blow you up."

"That's right."

"You escaped, he gave you a ride to Memphis, and fell in love with you on the two-hour drive."

"It was ninety minutes."

"I stand corrected. Decker fell in love with you in the space of ninety minutes and asked you to share his life."

"I never said Decker was in love with me. But yes, he asked me to share his life."

"You must be one helluva woman."

She wriggles out of her skin-tight pants and says, "I'll let *you* decide if I am."

Chapter 18

YOU PROBABLY WANT to know what happened after Jill pulled her pants down and made her very persuasive argument in favor of saving the United States from a despicable reign of terror. I'd like to tell you, but some things are better left unsaid.

Take what you know about me, and believe the best or worst. The issue was pretty simple: be faithful to Callie or protect the United States from terrorism.

What would *you* have done? Would *you* agree to a last fling with an incredibly sexy person in order to catch a dangerous terrorist? Or would you say, "I'm in love, and being unfaithful even one time—for any reason—is too much to ask. Especially if it means hurting the person I adore."

In a perfect world, people would always do the honorable thing. But which is more honorable: being faithful to my girlfriend or being faithful to my country?

It's best you don't know what happened next. Don't you agree?

Chapter 19

I'M JUST FUCKING with you.

I'd never keep you in the dark. We've been together too many years for that. I'll tell you what happened, as I always do, and take my chances on whether you like me more, or less, after knowing the details.

So Jill pulled her pants down...

...And I was very respectful, meaning I waited for her to remove her pants completely before responding. In the spirit of full disclosure, I will confirm she removed her panties, as well.

I can honestly say at that moment I had no intention of having sex with Jill, but neither was I insensitive to her feelings. In other words, I allowed her to remove her top, since that appeared to be her sincere wish.

I wasn't completely without restraint. I said, "Feel free to keep your high heels on."

With everyone out of the car except the two of us, there was plenty of room for Jill to lie down on the side seat, on her back, with her legs bent, spread wide apart.

"You make a great case for infidelity," I said, "and you've given me the closest thing to a last fling I'll ever have. But–"

"You can't find it in your heart to make love to me?"

"No. But if it matters, a week ago I'd have been all over you like whiskers on a Robertson."

"Will you watch me?"

"Uh...you don't mean...?"

"Yes. That's exactly what I mean."

"Quick question before you start?"

"Go ahead."

"From a woman's point of view, if I watch you, would I be cheating?"

"No."

"Can you give me a little more to go on?"

"You're killing the mood here, Donovan. You know that, right?"

"Sorry."

She sighs. "For the sake of argument, let's say you're home, and you look out the window and see a dog licking its pussy."

"There's a visual I wasn't expecting."

"The dog was going to lick it whether you watched or not, right?"

"Right."

"So that's not cheating. On the other hand, if you go outside and lick the dog's pussy, that would be cheating."

"Thanks for clearing that up."

"May I continue?"

"Why not? I'm just in my home, looking out the window."

I can understand how some among you might think that watching Jill pleasure herself is akin to cheating. But did I touch her?

No.

Did I encourage her?

No.

Am I *required* to discourage her?

That's the question.

I thought of lots of examples why it wasn't cheating to watch Jill murmur and moan and move around on the seat a few feet in front of me, pelvis gyrating, breasts undulating softly to the rhythmic rise and fall of her hips....

I thought about how the gift of eyesight is one of life's greatest treasures, and one that should be enjoyed to the fullest extent. I mean, who among you could turn away from a gorgeous sunset, an adorable baby, or a litter of newborn puppies? If these glorious views were placed before you by the gods of chance, wouldn't you be well within your rights to gaze and marvel at them?

Of course you would. So why should pussy be any different?

I'm not talking about viewing porn, or frequenting strip clubs. That's proactive viewing. In other words, there's a difference between chasing tornadoes and being home when a tornado strikes. If you're chasing pussy, you're cheating. I get that. But if pussy happens to strike less than five feet away, through no fault of your own, how can you be criticized for looking at it, any more than if a cute puppy suddenly came into view?

You love puppies, I love pussy. Which of us is worse?

You are.

Here's why: If you were sitting in my limo and a cute puppy happened to pop out of Jill's pants, you'd have your hands all over that pup within seconds. But when Jill's pussy popped out I never touched it once.

So run and tell that, homeboy.

But don't tell Callie, okay?

Chapter 20

Callie Carpenter.

I MUST BE slipping, Callie thinks, as she turns her car around and heads back to Kathleen's house.

In a million years she wouldn't have thought Kathleen would call Creed after being warned. Is the bitch really that stupid?

When Callie left Kathleen's house less than 20 minutes ago, Kathleen was pretty docile. But as she thought about Callie's visit, and what transpired, she must have gotten all worked up. The more she thought about it, the angrier—and braver—she became. She probably decided to tell Creed the whole story, and trusted him to protect her from Callie's wrath.

On the way back to Kathleen's house, Callie takes a moment to consider the consequences. With Kathleen dead,

Addie will be placed in foster care. That's not such a bad thing. Callie and Creed will do the research and find the best foster parents in the state.

But no. Addie deserves better.

Adoption's better.

Callie will make sure Addie gets adopted. She'll also set up a trust for Addie's education, medical expenses, and anything else she could ever want or need.

Problem solved.

Callie speeds up. She needs to get there before Kathleen leaves to fetch Addie from her friend's house.

Ten minutes later, at the edge of Kathleen's neighborhood, Callie parks her car, dons a hooded warm up jacket, and jogs to the house behind Kathleen's. She cuts through the yard and makes her way to Kathleen's garage, to the window she unlocked during her previous visit. She climbs inside, then calls Kathleen.

"Hello?"

"It's Callie."

"What do you want?"

"Are you still home?"

"No. I'm on my way to pick up Addie."

What a lying bitch! Her car's right here in the garage!

"Where are you, specifically?" Callie says. "I can meet you somewhere."

"I have to go."

She hangs up, and Callie hears her rushing through the house, toward the door that leads to the garage. Callie stuffs her phone in her back pocket, gets into position beside the door. When Kathleen rushes out, Callie grabs her by the arm and flings her to the floor. Kathleen screams, tries to scramble to her feet, but Callie gets a knee in her chest, and a thumb and forefinger on her throat.

Kathleen wants to speak, but can't. Her eyes are wide, pleading.

Callie says, "You knew what would happen. You've orphaned your daughter."

Chapter 21

THERE'S NOTHING CALLIE would like more than to tie this bitch up, strip her naked, and skin her alive. She'd give anything to make Kathleen suffer a long, slow death.

But Creed would know. He'd inspect her corpse and know she'd been tortured.

Moments ago she and Creed were talking about how one of the most humiliating things you can do to a cop is pull his pants down in public and write a message on his ass.

Assuming you don't want to physically harm him.

That's the difference, of course. Callie *does* intend to harm Kathleen. But can she torture her and somehow shift the blame?

Decker might be a good scapegoat. He obviously has some sort of connection to Creed. If he knows about Creed's ancestors, he surely knows about Kathleen.

What if Callie tortures Kathleen and writes BWC on her ass with a grease pen? Would Creed buy it?

Would Kathleen even *have* a grease pen?

Of course she would. She's a school teacher.

But there's a problem. Decker hasn't killed any civilians yet, so the crime wouldn't fit the pattern. Because of that, if Kathleen's death involves torture, Creed might suspect Callie. Much as she hates the idea, she needs to kill Kathleen quickly, and stage a robbery. A rape would be better, but where's a girl going to find a penis when she needs one?

She releases her grip on Kathleen's throat long enough to hear her blubbering something about her baby, but mostly she's trying to wriggle free of Callie's grip. That's not going to happen. Callie has years of fighting experience, and Kathleen's a frumpy school teacher.

"I warned you," Callie says. "I *warned* you!"

"*Please!*" Kathleen says. "We had a deal!"

"We did. But you fucked me over."

"It wasn't *me*! It was—"

Callie grips Kathleen's head with both hands and smashes it against the floor. It feels so good she does it again. And again and again till the back of Kathleen's head bursts like a ripe mellon.

On the floor, three feet away, Kathleen's cell phone rings.

The dial lights up. Callie sees a photo of Addie, who's trying to call her mom. Was, in fact, dialing her mom's number the very moment she was being murdered.

Callie feels a pang of remorse because Kathleen's death means Miranda Rodriguez—the mother of Creed's child—gets to live.

Which means she and Callie will be working together in a few short months.

Shit!

None of this would have happened if Kathleen hadn't called Creed. Why the fuck did she call him? They had a deal.

She stands and strips, enters Kathleen's house, takes a quick but thorough shower, picks out one of Kathleen's frumpy outfits, puts it on, and spends 15 minutes staging the crime scene. She puts her own bloody clothes in a plastic kitchen bag, climbs out the garage window, and walks to her car.

As she unlocks the car door it suddenly hits her.

Kathleen's cell phone will show she accepted a call from Callie's phone!

The phone call will have bounced off the nearest cell tower, and the cell phone record will place Callie right smack in the middle of the crime scene. The cops wouldn't know, of course, because her phone's encrypted. But Creed and his geeks would know.

How could she be so stupid?

More importantly, how can she fix it?

For starters, she needs to gain possession of Kathleen's cell phone. The cops could still obtain the records, but that will take time. And Callie only needs a few hours to locate and blow up the cell tower.

She hurries back to Kathleen's garage, but finds an empty spot where Kathleen's phone should be. She doesn't go crazy, searching all through the garage and house like some maniac. She doesn't do that because she knows she never touched the phone. And because she saw it a few minutes ago while staging the crime scene.

She's well aware someone took it.

But who?

Her own cell phone rings.

She pulls it from her back pocket, checks the screen, recognizes the caller.

It's Kathleen.

She glances at Kathleen's body.

The caller's clearly not Kathleen. But it *is* her cell phone.

Callie answers.

"Miss Carpenter, I hope I haven't caught you at a bad time."

"Who *is* this?"

"Ryan Decker."

"What do you want?"

"Right down to business. I like that."

"Like you said, you caught me at a bad time."

"Very well, I'll get straight to the point. I want you to join my urban army."

"In return for?"

"Keeping your secret."

"About?"

"Meeting with Kathleen today. And killing her just now."

Callie frowns. "Call me back in ten minutes."

Decker says, "You're hanging *up* on me? Seriously?"

Chapter 22

CALLIE HANGS UP on Decker and searches the garage till she finds the pinhole camera. She rips it out, shoves it in her pocket. She'd like to search the house, but knows her time is limited. The lady keeping Addie will eventually show up, or have a neighbor check to see if Kathleen's home.

Callie goes to the kitchen, searches the drawers till she finds an indelible marker. It's not a grease pen, but it'll get the job done. She carefully approaches Kathleen's corpse, taking great pains not to step in the pooled blood.

Kathleen's lying on her back.

That's good because Callie can unbutton her jeans and pull her pants and panties to her knees. But it's also bad news, because she's been dead long enough that the coroner will be able to tell she was turned over long after the murder.

Wait. Could that work to her advantage? Maybe it'll convince the cops there was more than one perpetrator, or that the crime scene was contaminated by a second person thirty minutes after Kathleen's death. It might create loose ends that could send the investigation in a number of different directions.

Another good thing is the blood has pooled around Kathleen's head, and not so much beneath her torso. By working slowly and carefully, Callie should be able to flip her onto her stomach without getting blood on her own clothes—meaning the clothes she stole from Kathleen.

She pulls Kathleen's pants and panties down to her ankles and stares at her crotch for a full minute, especially the area Creed calls her vertical smile. What she's thinking, Creed's been here. He's spent many happy hours in this bronze-tufted triangle, and liked it. And because he enjoyed it so much, Kathleen's dead.

And there's a video somewhere that proves Callie killed her.

And Ryan Decker has it.

She stares at Kathleen's crotch some more and starts fuming. It's all she can do not to mutilate her. Of course Kathleen would be stupid enough not to notice the hidden cameras, and of course Decker saw and recorded everything. The meeting this afternoon, her threats, their kissing...

Is Callie slipping? Should she have thought to check for cameras?

No.

There was no reason to suspect this mundane school teacher had been targeted by Decker, or anyone else. And Callie knew nothing about Decker till this morning.

It just happened.

173

She keeps her cool, figures she'll deal with Decker when he calls, and do all she can in the meantime to mitigate her mistakes. She starts by flipping Kathleen facedown, so she can write BWC on her ass.

Except that...when she flips her over she sees...*Kathleen already has BWC written on her ass!*

With a grease pen.

But how?

Callie thinks a minute. Kathleen died on her back. Decker couldn't have turned her over to write on her ass after the fact. If he had, Kathleen's forehead and face would have been smeared with blood.

And they weren't.

He wrote BWC on her ass *before* she died. Which means he was in Kathleen's house when Callie killed her. He must have paid Kathleen a visit after Callie left the first time. Then wrote on her ass and forced her to call Creed, hoping Callie would come back to kill her.

Decker set them up. Orchestrated the whole thing. Delivered Kathleen to her death. Not that it matters now, but Kathleen may have intended to stick to their deal, which means Decker's a formidable foe. He tricked Callie, used her, and now he owns her.

Callie's phone rings.

"It's been ten minutes," Decker says. "And I've lost my video feed to Kathleen's garage. Any idea how that happened?"

"Why did you write BWC on her ass?"

"You found that? Good for you. I did it to prove I'm willing to take credit for her death if I have to. And I will, if you agree to work with me."

"What would I have to do?"

"Two things. First, agree to never help find or kill me. Second, convince Creed to accept my demands."

Callie pauses. "That's it?"

"That's it."

"Why don't I believe you?"

"Because you know I could use this against you in so many ways."

"Why aren't you?"

Decker laughs. "After seeing you naked on camera just now, it was extremely hard not to demand sex."

"Why didn't you? I would have done it."

"I know. But please don't say that again, because I find you stunningly attractive, and it's already eating me alive. Not taking advantage of you is something I'll probably regret for a long time."

"Well, if it means anything, I appreciate it. Very much."

He pauses. "It means a lot, Miss Carpenter. Please know I have the utmost respect for you and Mr. Creed, and have no desire to blackmail you or harm your chances for happiness. For me this is about the money, nothing more."

"Since you broached the subject, how much are you demanding?"

"Don't laugh. A billion dollars."

"That seems awfully high for a guy who writes graffiti on people's asses."

"I agree. Which is why I need your help getting Creed to say yes."

"Creed will do what he thinks is right."

"Of course. But if he happens to ask your advice?"

"I'll tell him to pay the money."

"Good girl. And the other part?"

"I'm in. You have my word. I won't help them find or kill you."

"Good."

"What's your backup plan?"

"If Creed says no, I'll have to take my case to the public. Unfortunately, lives will have to be lost before the media takes me seriously."

"Of course. So. What happens now?"

"After you leave, my people will hustle over to Kathleen's garage and clean the crime scene."

"And the body?"

"—Will never be found."

"And her cell phone?"

"—Is already in your rental car."

"And the cell tower records?"

"Hopefully you can do something about that. But the tower itself will be gone by midnight."

"And the videos you made of me and Kathleen?"

"I hope you'll understand why I need to keep those."

"Insurance."

"Exactly. If something happens to me, the tapes will go public around the world. But please believe that will never happen unless you go back on your word."

"I believe you."

"Thanks. That also means a lot to me."

Callie finds Kathleen's cell phone in the console of her rental car. She removes the battery, puts it in her handbag, and checks into a different hotel, using a name and ID Creed has never heard of. She changes clothes, leaves the hotel, drives a few miles, tosses the clothes she borrowed from Kathleen into a dumpster. Then she drives back to the hotel, goes to her room, orders room service. While waiting for her dinner to arrive, she puts the battery back in Kathleen's phone and investigates the contents. Sees the photos of Addie she expected to find. Checks the text messages, finds nothing strange or unusual. She hooks the phone up to her computer, runs a scan on the deleted photos, and sees something that turns her world upside down.

Chapter 23

KATHLEEN'S CELL PHONE contains recently deleted photos of Donovan Creed!

In this one he's lying in bed, sleeping. In this one he's completely nude, with his back to the camera, walking toward Kathleen's bathroom. In this one, he's sideways, taking a shower. In this one, a close up of his penis is taking a shower. Creed seems completely oblivious to the photos being shot, and normally Callie wouldn't make a big deal out of a former girlfriend capturing private moments of her lover and his anatomy on a disk years ago, even if the former girlfriend decided to keep the photos for her personal enjoyment.

Except that when Kathleen was dating Creed, he had a different face.

These photos show his current face. The one Kathleen was supposed to have seen for the first time at dinner last night. Now that Callie thinks about it, when Kathleen greeted Creed she said, "Hello, Donovan." What she should have said was, "Nice face!" or, "I never would have believed it was you!" But she didn't make any comment about his face.

Doesn't that seem strange?

It does, now that Callie thinks about it.

How did she fail to pick up on it last night while listening to their conversation?

Simple. She wasn't expecting Kathleen to be at the dinner. She was expecting a possible ambush. Then she got sidetracked by Rose and the very pregnant Miranda.

Callie's the first to admit she jumps to conclusions. But these photos aren't an example of her imagination running wild. They're camera specific. They weren't transferred from Kathleen's original iPhone. They were taken from her iPhone 5.

They didn't have iPhone 5's when Kathleen and Creed were dating.

Not to mention these particular photos are time-and-date stamped, which proves they were taken eight weeks ago. Which means Creed fucked Kathleen exactly two days before Callie told him she loved him and made the decision to share his life.

Callie feels the rush of boiling blood flooding her system. Feels the adrenalin kick in. She stands and flips her desk over. Throws a chair across the room so hard it smashes against the wall. She reaches for the standing lamp but hears her cell phone vibrate. She glances at the display and sees that Decker has sent her a video attachment.

Callie's not in the mood to watch a video. She'd rather trash her room and kill whoever bangs on the wall to complain about it. She picks up the mangled chair and smashes it repeatedly against the wall.

No one complains.

The fucking chair has been reduced to kindling and no one's complaining about the *noise*? What's the *matter* with people?

She opens the door that connects to the adjoining room. As expected, there's a second door locked from the other side. One kick to the left of the lock is all it takes to weaken the frame. Two more kicks and she's in.

Someone got lucky. The room is vacant.

She looks around. What would an angry rock star do?

Trash the room.

She grabs the desk chair and flings it into the giant-screen TV. Tries to lift the bed, but finds it bolted. She screams in frustration. Then spots the floor-to-ceiling window, and decides to take her life.

She throws herself full speed into the window, expecting to crash through and plummet to her death, but—*damn it to hell!*—it's safety glass. The impact makes the whole room shudder, but the glass holds, and Callie rebounds painfully to the floor. She lies there a moment, on her side, then rolls onto her back. Her chest is heaving with violent intentions.

This would be a bad time for someone to complain about the noise.

A very bad time.

She wonders why no one's called the front desk. That's how it works, right? Some asshole tears up a room at night, guests call the front desk to complain, the front desk calls the room to warn or threaten them...

If someone working the front desk calls she might go downstairs and create a bloodbath.

She pictures herself vaulting over the front desk counter, slashing throats, going from one office to the next, slaughtering employees and managers alike.

There are few sounds Callie enjoys more than a razor-sharp blade slicing through a meaty section of human flesh. But one is the initial strike of a non-fatal stab. In order for the sound to be right, the knife must enter the body all the way to the front quillon without hitting ribs, bones, or vital organs. If you plan to stab someone for the sheer enjoyment of hearing the sound, you need to know anatomy and strike angles, because it's harder than you think to stab a human with a proper knife and not hit bone.

Callie has a proper knife.

And the knowledge and desire to use it.

She hears a small chirp from the next room that reminds her Decker sent her a video file.

She gets to her feet, walks to her room, clicks on the file and sees a short video of a recent rally, where an unseen Decker instructs his troops in the use of spray cans to render policemen and park visitors unconscious. He explains how they need to work in teams. Four per cop, three per civilian. One distracts the target, one sprays the target's face, one or two catch the targets as they fall. One pulls the pants down, one writes BWC on the ass.

What makes the video unique, it wasn't made before the Central Park attack. And the troops aren't college-aged men.

They're college-aged women.

And the attack is scheduled for 9:00 a.m. tomorrow, in Jackson Square, New Orleans, less than a mile from the Rose Dumont Hotel, where Creed is staying tonight.

It's a test.

Callie's so pissed about Creed's affair with Kathleen she has half a mind to warn him about the impending Jackson Square attack. If she does, Decker will send Creed the video of her killing Kathleen. The question is, does Callie really care if Creed finds out?

She thinks about it.

Yes, she *does* care.

Because she's won.

True, Creed never told her he'd been sleeping with Kathleen, but fucking Kathleen doesn't necessarily mean he had feelings for her. What really counts is two days after the photos were taken, when Callie said she wanted to be with him, he said yes and dumped Kathleen.

Callie now realizes killing Kathleen was the right thing to do. She would have been a perpetual threat to their happiness, because couples argue. It's unavoidable. If Creed had kept Kathleen in his back pocket, he might have contacted her during the tough times. If Callie and Creed had a verbal or physical argument at some point, it would be human nature for Creed to seek comfort with the woman who loved and adored him all these years.

And she would have spread her legs for him without a moment's hesitation.

But Kathleen is no longer an option for Creed. No future threat to their relationship.

Ding Dong, the witch is dead!

Callie will keep Decker's upcoming attack a secret. And why not? What's the big deal about park visitors getting some grease on their asses? If Decker can wrangle a billion dollars for what amounts to a college prank, more power to him. And if Creed somehow finds out that Callie killed Kathleen, maybe that won't be such a big deal, either. Creed had to know he couldn't have possibly made a life with that nagging frump. If Creed finds out, Callie will apologize, promise never to kill his other girlfriends, and eventually, he'll forgive her.

Because Callie's going to be the best girlfriend he ever had.

If she can get over the fact he was fucking Kathleen behind her back.

She calls Decker and says, "Nice video."

"Thanks. Are you still on board?"

"Yes. Can I ask you something?"

"Of course."

"Where's Kathleen?"

He pauses. "You don't expect me to answer that, do you?"

"Yes."

"Over the phone?"

"Yes."

"Why do you want to know?"

"I need closure."

He laughs. "You're something else. Stay tuned."

Two minutes later Callie's phone chirps with a text message.

Chapter 24

THE DISPLAY ON Callie's phone shows the call came from a different cell phone. Obviously a disposable, untraceable, pre-paid one, which makes sense, given the message: *Fresh, Shallow Grave,* and the coordinates, which shows Kathleen's body is located 80 miles from Callie's hotel.

She quickly packs her clothes, a sheet, and her personal items, and heads down the hall toward the elevators. On the way, she nods at the security cop who's heading to her room to complain about the noise.

If only he'd come sooner.

Another lucky bastard gets to live another day.

Callie takes the elevator to the parking garage, loads the coordinates into her GPS, and follows the verbal directions. When the voice says, "You have arrived at your destination," she leaves her headlights on and walks 11 yards before finding the mound of dirt where Kathleen's buried. She places the sheet on the lower half of the mound and lies on it.

Then takes her knife and plunges it into the center of the mound.

And feels nothing.

Not so shallow after all.

She stands, pulls the sheet away, looks for the shovel they would have left at the scene after removing any finger prints. Decker's people would be smart enough to know you don't transport a dead body in a vehicle, and then keep the shovel that dug the grave. Because if for some reason they were stopped by a cop, the shovel could lead to questions that could be answered by a cadaver-sniffing dog, followed by a soil analysis that could match them to the grave site.

She finds the shovel and digs up enough dirt to expose Kathleen's body. Then she places the sheet on the bottom half of Kathleen's corpse, lies down on it, and methodically stabs every square inch of Kathleen's body above the waist. Then she stands, moves the sheet to the base of the grave, and says, "I don't like you, Kathleen. And I never will."

She lies down on the sheet and begins stabbing Kathleen's crotch. After a dozen hard strikes, her cell phone rings.

She answers, "Funny you should call, Donovan."

"Why's that?"

"I was just thinking of you."

"This very moment?"

"Yup."

"Is that why you sound out of breath?"

"Yup."

"Cool. What were you thinking?"

"Sexual thoughts."

Chapter 25

Donovan Creed.

THIS MORNING, AT 9:00 a.m. Decker struck Jackson Square with college-aged women!

Law enforcement throughout the country had been concentrating on college-aged men carrying backpacks in parks and other public areas.

Up north, the U.W. Oshkosh Glee Club was arrested en masse while setting up for a scheduled public performance at the local amphitheater. Down south, an unfortunate dance troupe was attacked and savagely beaten at an outdoor mall in Brighton, Georgia, by a pack of primitive rednecks.

No one suspected women.

Not even me.

And now I'm on the phone with Ryan Decker, who's demanding—try to contain yourself—a billion dollars to stop the attacks.

"Why me?" I say.

"What do you mean?"

"Why tell *me* your demands, instead of the press, the police, or some government official?"

"Few people understand the implications of what I've accomplished the past two days. Fewer still have the ability to conceive what lies ahead."

"But you think I do?"

"I'm certain of it."

"I don't even exist, as far as the government's concerned."

"Maybe not, but I happen to know you've got the president's ear, which gives us a decent chance to orchestrate a happy ending for all concerned. By keeping my demands private, we can avoid a wide-spread panic."

"It won't work."

"I agree the chances are slim. But if anyone can prevent the carnage, it's you."

"You'll need to come down on your price."

"A billion *is* a bargain."

"They won't pay that."

"Then I'll have to take my case to the public."

"The problem with that, you'll outrage the country. You want them scared, not angry."

"Those who live will be plenty scared."

"We'll eventually catch you."

"It's inevitable. And I'd rather not be caught. But I'm well-prepared. I think I can make an impact."

"I think so too." I pause, then say, "I'll call my boss, see what he has to say."

"I appreciate that."

"What's your deadline?"

"I don't believe in deadlines. If I say noon tomorrow, they'll wait to see if I actually do something at noon tomorrow. If I do, it'll be harder for them to justify paying me. If I don't, I'll be perceived as weak. Tell you what: I'll call *you* at noon tomorrow and see how it's going."

"Sounds fair."

"I know you're obligated to set up all your equipment in an attempt to trace the call tomorrow, to try to locate me. I understand that. It won't work, but you have to go through the motions. That's what sucks about being a bureaucrat. Common sense goes out the window. What a colossal waste of time."

"How do you want it?"

"What?"

"The money."

"Are you hopeful I'll actually get paid?"

"No. But I'll make a strong case."

"Thanks. I respect you for that. But I won't waste your time with details about how to deliver money that hasn't been collected yet. If it's a yes, we'll have plenty of time to work things out."

"Can I ask you a question?"

"Go ahead."

"Do I know you?"

"I think not. If you did, you'd recognize me from the sketch that's being shown all over the world."

"Is it a good likeness?"

"I'd rather not say. Who provided the description?"

"I'd rather not say."

"Fair enough. Bye for now."

"Wait."

"Please tell me you're not trying to trace *this* call."

"No. But I *am* recording it."

"Of course you are."

"I have enough to try to match your voice prints."

"I'd expect nothing less."

"Thanks. Actually, I'm curious about your connection to Emmett Love."

"He's your ancestor."

"I've got lots of ancestors."

"Me too."

He hangs up, leaving me to wonder what he meant. Could he and I be related somehow?

I think about calling my geeks to see if they can establish a detailed family tree going back to the pre-Emmett Love era, to see if there were any Deckers in my ancestry. Then decide against it. I doubt Ryan Decker's his real name, and I don't want to divert my geeks from trying to locate him.

I call Sherm Phillips, U.S. Secretary of Defense.

"What's up?" Sherm says.

"You been keeping up with this BWC foolishness?"

"Who hasn't? It's a bigger story than Reese Witherspoon's new hair color."

"We can make it go away for a billion dollars."

He laughs. "Tell Decker to keep scribbling on asses."

"The grease pen's just the beginning. He's been planning this a long time. He'll remain several steps ahead of us. He'll escalate the attacks."

"We've got his picture, and from what I understand, your geeks should have his complete profile within hours. He's got no chance."

"How many years did it take to catch Bin Laden?"

"He was in a different country. We'll find Decker sooner, not later."

"I agree. But he's going to do a lot of damage in the meantime."

"It's a no on the money. You know our position. We don't deal with terrorists."

"Not officially. But it wouldn't be the first time we've paid one off."

"The price for ass painting is far less than bombing buildings."

"He bombed some lake houses."

"Child's play."

"Will you run it by the president?"

He pauses. "Please tell me you're not recommending we pay this joker."

"That's exactly what I'm recommending. If we don't nip it now, it's going to get ugly."

"He pulls people's pants down! You know who else does that? Clowns! This guy's a clown. I can't believe you want to pay him."

"He knows what he's doing."

"Where's the proof of that?"

"Could you coordinate an attack on three policemen and more than thirty civilians in Central Park in broad daylight without being seen or photographed by a single witness?"

"If I had 100 guys? Why not?"

"How do you find 100 college-age guys to do that? And how do you teach them to post the photos on social media in such a way that the photos can't be traced back to them?"

"The president doesn't consider this a serious threat. If Decker wants a deal tell him to come back at me with a hundred grand. Hell, make it a buck-fifty. But a billion dollars? A *billion*?" He laughs again. "Tell him to fuck off."

"I'll tell him. But don't say I didn't warn you."

"Noted. Call me when you've got some hard facts on the guy."

We hang up and I call Callie. When she answers I say, "Guess who I just spoke to."

"Kathleen?"

"Ryan Decker."

"No shit? What did he want?"

"He made me an offer."

"Why *you*?"

"I asked him the same question."

"And?"

"He thinks I've got the president's ear. Thinks if we negotiate in private he'll have a better chance to get paid."

"How much is he asking for?"

"Guess."

"Ten million."

"That's high, don't you think?"

"Not really."

"A billion."

"Excuse me?"

"He's demanding a billion dollars."

Callie laughs. "*That* seems high. What did you say?"

"I told him I'd make a few calls."

"Think they'll pay?"

"Would you?"

"If *I'm* president? Of course. Because I wouldn't want to be remembered as the one who could have stopped it, but didn't. Have they caught any of the women?"

"Nope. No photographs, no evidence. Pretty damned hard to accomplish in the age of cell phone cameras, don't you think?"

"I think Decker's ex-military. Or ex-CIA."

"Could be. Even though it was a bullshit attack—grease pens on asses—it was organized and executed with military precision."

"What about Jill?"

"What about her?"

"Last night you were planning to have her call Decker."

"I changed my mind."

"Why?"

"Too quick. Too obvious. I'd like to save her for later. Keep her under wraps a bit longer. Maybe I'll get lucky."

"*Excuse* me?"

"Maybe Decker will contact her personally, and I won't have to work the whole thing out. What did you *think* I meant?"

"I wasn't sure. But after hearing how every man who meets her falls in love—"

"Don't be silly. You've got nothing to worry about. If she stripped naked four feet in front of me I wouldn't even touch her."

"Would you look at her?"

I laugh. "That's an odd question."

"*Would* you?"

"What do *you* think?"

"I think you would."

"And would that bother you?"

"Immensely. In fact, I'd never get over it."

"Then I'll make sure not to look, should the occasion ever arise."

"Thanks, Donovan."

"I had another reason for calling. I want you to come to New Orleans this afternoon."

"Why?"

"We're going to kill Bobby DiPiese."

"Who, you and me?"

"And Joe, though he'll be off-site when we go in."

"Tonight?"

"Yup. I'm gathering supplies as we speak."

"You'll send a jet?"

"It's already waiting for you at Teterboro."

"Are we done in New York City?"

"Why do you ask?"

"I need to know if I should bring all my clothes, or keep them here and extend my stay."

"Keep the room at the Plaza. If all goes well we'll fly back after the job tonight."

"Okay. Except that I'm not at the Plaza. I'm at the Peninsula."

"Why'd you change hotels?"

"The Plaza's on the edge of Central Park."

"So?"

"I was afraid someone would knock me down and write on my ass. And only you get to do that."

I laugh.

She says, "Speaking of assholes, what about Kathleen?"

"That's rather harsh. What about her?"

"We were planning to call her tonight."

"I'll call her now, if you like."

"I want to be with you when you talk to her. I want to hear her say she understands you're taken."

"She already knows that. But okay, if that's what you want."

"It is. Thanks. I'll see you soon." She pauses. Then says, "I love you."

"Thanks for adding that. I love you, too, Callie."

"Don't ever stop." She pauses again. Then says, "Or else."

I laugh, and hang up.

Then realize she didn't share the laugh.

PART THREE:
Getting to Yes

Chapter 1

Donovan Creed.

TWO WEEKS AGO Ryan Decker demanded a billion dollars to stop writing on asses.

I wasn't happy about Sherm's decision two weeks ago, and I'm not happy about it now.

Of course, Sherm's gloating.

"Where's the attack you were expecting?" he asks. "Like I said, Decker's a clown. It was all a big bluff."

I disagree. Decker's face and physical description have been shown on every TV news program, newspaper, and magazine in the country. Every day we're hearing new stories, but no one seems to have an idea about him or where he is.

Not that there aren't leads.

Decker sightings are coming in faster than lies from a politician. The screening system is so backed up it'll take the FBI years to investigate everyone accused of being the Willow Lake Bomber.

I'm waiting for the other shoe to drop, while mourning Kathleen. Quietly, because Callie has jealousy issues where Kathleen is concerned. Let me catch you up: Two weeks ago Kathleen went missing. I only heard about it a few days ago, when Curly told me he was sorry it happened.

"How could you not know she's been missing for two *weeks?*" I shouted. "You're supposed to keep up with these things!"

He's not, though, and neither are the other geeks. No part of their job description involves keeping up with my former girlfriends, though they tend to do it on their own time.

Curly felt awful being yelled at, and I felt awful for yelling at him. The Geeks have no love lives, and tend to live vicariously through mine. Upon meeting them, I was surprised to learn they had each picked one of my girlfriends to call their own. Larry's favorite is Callie. C.H. favors Miranda. And Curly has always loved Kathleen. He would've found out about her much sooner, but I've been pushing them day and night to locate Ryan Decker.

To no avail.

If *they* can't find him, the guy is good.

And I fear the country will know that fairly soon. Decker's about to make his move. I can *feel* it.

When I told him the government refused to pay, Decker took it in stride. Didn't get angry, didn't make idle threats. He simply thanked me for trying, and wished me good luck and good health.

And I haven't heard from him since.

The cops have nothing on Kathleen's disappearance, so I hired a team of private detectives to look into the matter. Their first job was to find Addie. That took ten minutes. She's staying with a friend. I called the mom and asked if there was anything I could do. She said no, but took my name and number and promised to call if she hears anything. I promised to do the same.

I'm not a mopey guy, but Kathleen was special to me. If Callie hadn't revealed her feelings toward me when she did, I was on the verge of rekindling a relationship with Kathleen. When Jill asked if I could remember the name of my last fling I said, "The last one I slept with or the last one I cared about?" She said the last one I slept with.

The truth is, I remember both.

The last one I cared about was Kathleen. The last one I slept with was Faith Stallone, from Louisville, Kentucky.

I slept with both women back to back, eight weeks ago, a couple of days before Callie told me she loved me.

Not at the same time, but on the same day.

I hooked up with Kathleen when I went to visit Doctor Box about Callie's recovery. Addie was spending the night with a friend, and Kathleen overwhelmed me at the door. I was in town, thinking of her, and in a moment of weakness decided to call to tell her I was alive, and to check up on her. As it turned out, she already knew I was alive. She begged me to come over for a drink. It was late, one drink became several, and we wound up in bed. I fell asleep, got up the next morning, showered, kissed her goodbye, and left.

That afternoon I flew to Cincinnati to meet mob boss Sal Bonadello. We chatted a few hours, during which he gave me the names of a couple of mobsters he wanted me to kill. After an early dinner, I checked into the nicest hotel in town, freshened up, and hit the bar downstairs to sip some bourbon.

Moments later I found myself ordering a drink for the hot thirty-something sitting by herself in the corner booth.

She loved my fake face and jade-green eyes. Was thoroughly convinced I was that movie star guy. I told her yeah, I get that all the time. Then I compared her to a famous actress, which didn't hurt her mood in the least. I started to introduce myself, but she stopped me and said, "I'm just going to call you Movie Man." She invited me to sit. I noticed her wedding ring and asked where her husband was. She said he was meeting a client, and hadn't bothered calling to say he was running late, which was par for the course.

"Everything's about Jake," she said, which is why she invited me to sit with her.

"I want him to see me having a drink with someone who looks like you," she said. "I want him to see us laughing, having a great time."

Then she started crying.

Turns out she believed Jake may have been cheating on her.

I liked the way she looked and told her so, and pointed out there's nothing in the world more satisfying than revenge sex. It took a couple of drinks and my best smile to get her into the men's room for what I thought would be a quick-and-sloppy, but she wound up fucking my eyes out. Afterward, back at the table she was reeling.

"Oh, my God!" she said. "That was the best sex of my life."

"Thanks," I said.

She laughed. "It had nothing to do with you, Movie Man."

"How could you have the best sex of your life and claim it had nothing to do with me?""Like you said, it was all about the revenge. I kept thinking, 'Oh my God, I'm in the men's room! What if Jake comes in to pee?' I pictured him walking in and seeing me bent over a filthy sink getting pounded from behind by a total stranger with movie star looks. I kept imagining the expression on his face and wanted him to see how good his wife can grind when she's got a good enough reason."

"Well, I'm glad I happened along when I did," I said, publicly humble, while privately proud to have given a bitchy woman the fuck of her life. Just for the record, Faith was not the best sex I ever had. But she was by far the best I ever had in a men's room.

I tried turning it into a compliment. "You were the best I ever had—"

"Who cares?" she said.

—I decided not to finish the sentence.

Faith said, "This proves one thing, though."

"What's that?"

"It proves I can survive outside marriage. It proves I've still got it."

I nodded, and asked if she still wanted me to hang around till Jake showed up.

"No, I'm good," she said.

"Want my real name?"

"No thanks."

"Can I get your phone number?"

"I think not."

I stood, bowed, and left her there.

Chapter 2

I'M IN CALLIE'S penthouse in Vegas, thinking about Kathleen, worrying about Addie. I have a strong feeling Kathleen isn't coming back. Police say Addie was the last person to see her alive, aside from her abductor, and the mom of a fellow student was the last to hear from her. I spoke to both and got nothing.

They found Kathleen's car several days ago at the airport. There were no prints in or on the car. No fibers, or evidence of any kind. No purse, cell phone, or personal effects.

Police can't pull her most recent cell phone records because the cell tower blew up the same evening Kathleen went missing. The towers use data sharing, and the records are certain to exist somewhere, but without Kathleen's phone it will be hard to isolate the most recent information in a useful way. And even if the data is recovered I doubt the records will provide any leads. I think the best they can hope for is to learn where her phone was before the battery was disconnected.

Callie and I think Decker may have abducted her. That might explain the cell tower explosion, though I'm not sure why such a severe measure would be necessary to cover up a kidnapping. But if Decker's responsible, there's an outside chance he's holding her hostage.

And yet, I can't shake the feeling she's dead.

I hook up my cell phone to Callie's stereo system and press the keys that take me to the one Roy Orbison song I own.

Growing up, I never "got" Roy's voice. Didn't appreciate it. I considered him sort of weird, and a little creepy. To me, his voice was strange and all over the place.

Then, years ago, I heard him sing *A Love So Beautiful*.

By then I was older, had more life experiences. My appreciation for music had widened to include opera. My favorite? *Nessun Dorma*, an aria from Puccini's *Turandot*.

In November, 1988, Jeff Lynne, the genius behind ELO, produced a solo album for Roy, one month before Roy died of a heart attack. A track from that album, written by Roy and Jeff, was inspired by *Nessun Dorma*.

It's titled, *A Love So Beautiful*.

I'm still not a big fan of Roy's, but this timeless tribute to lost love is something special. Roy's heartbroken, middle-aged voice soars with emotion, beauty, and grace. It may be the greatest love song ever written and performed.

But it's not for the young, or the casual listener. It should be heard with closed eyes, and might require two or three plays to feel the pain.

Roy nails it, of course. His life was filled with tragedy and sorrow. Family members claim the only time they ever saw Roy cry was the day he listened to the studio playback of *A Love So Beautiful*, because it spoke to his heart.

I'm terribly saddened, but not heartsick over losing Kathleen. We had our time, and moved on, and shared a special night two months ago, and moved on again. But anytime a beautiful young woman dies it's a tragedy, especially when she leaves behind a young daughter.

Yes, there's an outside chance Kathleen's alive.

But it's a small one.

I never played Roy's song for her, but I'm playing it now, while sipping bourbon. I think she would have enjoyed it. If she turns up alive, I'll send her a copy. If not, the next 3:33 is for her.

I play the song, thinking of my special moments with Kathleen, and when it's done, I put my feelings for her in a little box in the attic of my brain.

Then I press repeat, and play the song for me.

As it hits the halfway mark, Callie enters the room and says, "How much whiskey does it take to make that shit sound like music?"

I start to say something, then laugh, instead.

Ah, youth.

I've lost that, too.

Chapter 3

"YOU'RE IN A funk," Callie says. "You know what I do when I'm in a funk?"

"Kill people?"

"Besides that."

I think a minute. I have no idea what Callie does with her spare time, other than kill people. I wonder what that says about our relationship.

It definitely calms Callie to kill people, and to a lesser extent, I'm the same way. It's in our blood. The problem with killing people when you're in a funk, it's so easy. Almost too easy. If it weren't for our victims, you could make the case Callie and I are serial killers. Wait. That didn't come out right. Here's what I mean: except for gangland hits, our murders almost always involve suspected or proven terrorists. We make the occasional mistake, and collateral damage occurs from time to time, but our intentions are usually good. For us, it's a numbers game. If we've killed a dozen by mistake, the hundred we killed on purpose prevented the deaths of thousands.

When Jill Whittaker-DiPiese told me I could delay the killing of her husband, I figured out a way to save most, if not all, the prisoners in their basement. Two weeks ago Callie and I went to Bobby's house with that very intention. Had we killed him and his goons, and saved the prisoners, Callie's right, I'd be in a better mood.

But we didn't.

Everything seemed perfect. Joe Penny rigged up a couple of flash bombs to create a diversion. The plan? The first bomb goes off in the far corner of the backyard. The bad guys run outside to fight or take cover, facing the area of attack. One minute later, two additional bombs detonate. One in the backyard, much closer to the house, and a small one designed to blow the side door open. If all goes well, the bad guys don't hear the side door explosion. Callie and I walk through that door, search out and shoot the bad guys using super-soakers filled with cyanogen gas.

Cyanogen causes histotoxic anemia, and a quick death for anyone we hit. The gas is effective, but tricky. Standard protocol requires a double antidote, so we typically ingest sodium thiosulphate before the attack, and amyl nitrate when fumes are present.

Prior to attacking, Callie and I took the sodium thiosulphate, as prescribed. But as luck would have it, my supplier screwed up on the amyl nitrate. No problem, there are other ways to achieve a secondary antidote. I started things off by saying, "Wish I hadn't eaten asparagus three hours ago."

Callie said, "Turn on your night vision goggles so you can see my expression."

She showed me a sour look and her middle finger. Then said, "You planned this. Lucky for you we're dating."

"Lucky in every possible way."

She said, "I'll take a wild guess and assume you want to watch me do this?"

"How could I not?"

Callie squatted and peed into two handkerchiefs, and we tied them tightly to our faces. While not as effective as amyl nitrate, a urine-soaked handkerchief will serve as a secondary antidote for Cyanogen gas fumes.

So there we were. Bombs ready to explode, cyanogen gas weapons at the ready, night-vision goggles in place, urine-soaked handkerchiefs covering our faces....

The bombs went off on schedule, Callie and I burst through the side door....

But no one was home.

We checked the entire house and basement and found no evidence of prisoners, chains, or torture, but the scent of bleach was so strong in the basement we nearly passed out.

"I don't get it," I said. "There are six cars in the driveway."

"When did you think to check for people?" Callie said, with attitude.

"Four hours ago Joe reported six vans on the property, and numerous goons moving around inside the house. He came back an hour ago to set the timers. The vans and people were still on the property, and he made a positive ID of Bobby DiPiese."

"Someone at Baton Rouge PD must have alerted him earlier today. He and his goons probably spent the whole evening killing prisoners, scrubbing the place down. Lucky bastards must have loaded the vans with bodies and hauled ass minutes before we got here."

When you expect to kill goons and get a face full of urine instead, you tend to feel cheated.

I called Larry, the dwarf, and had him run a trace on Bobby, but after a couple of days he informed me Bobby had vanished, which means he's probably with Decker.

Now, in Vegas, Callie's staring at me.

What were we talking about?

Oh yeah. She asked if I knew what she does when she's in a funk.

Suddenly I remember something she likes to do. "You dance," I say.

She laughs. "Not when I'm feeling blue. And I certainly wouldn't recommend it as therapy for you, since you hate dancing more than anyone I ever met." She sighs. "Now that we're a couple I suppose I'll have to give it up."

"I'll dance with you on your birthdays," I say.

She gives me a questioning look, to see if I'm serious. When she realizes I am, her look changes to a level of joy that seems way out of context for such a simple concession on my part. Makes me glad I offered.

"You've surprised me," she says.

"I'm full of surprises. So tell me. What do you do when you're in a funk?"

"I buy shit," she says.

"Like what, clothes?"

"Clothes, cars, guns, electronics—whatever suits my pleasure."

She studies my face and posture and says, "But you're not much of a shopper. You'd probably prefer sex."

I smile. "Bingo!"

"Shall we to the bedroom go?" she says, with a song in her voice.

"Let's do," I say, rising to the occasion in two different ways.

"I've been practicing," she says.

"Uh oh."

"What's wrong?"

"I've been practicing? That's three words a boyfriend never likes to hear."

She laughs. "That came out wrong. What I mean is, I've been practicing in my mind."

"Good for you!"

"Wait. There's more!"

"Tell me."

"I watched some light porn without gagging. And took notes."

I don't comment, but I'm glad to hear she's working on it. Callie may not be great in bed, but I'd rather have bad sex with her than great sex with anyone else. I've never complained, and never will, but Callie knows she's been coming up short in the bedroom. Every time we have sex she promises to do a better job next time. It's not something I worry about. I'm okay with how things are. I know it's not easy for her, and I'm just so damned honored and grateful to be in bed with her at all.

Having said that, this time it's different.

She's kissing me differently. Touching me differently. Her movements are all out of character, but our bodies are synching better than ever before.

Let me explain.

Women like Callie don't make the best lovers. She's drop-dead gorgeous, and never had to learn how to please a man. On the other hand, women like Kathleen, who don't have runway model looks, take the time to learn how to kiss and move and satisfy a man in a way that transcends their looks. In public, Kathleen was cute, quiet, and practically nerdy. She wasn't athletic. But put her between two sheets and she turned into a panther.

Kathleen was a 10 in bed.

Callie's extremely athletic. Possibly too athletic to have great sex with a man. Or maybe I'm just saying that because she has a long history of preferring women to men. She and I both slept with Gwen Peters, a former stripper, and Gwen told me quite candidly that Callie is ten times the lover I am. So I know she's great with women. But with me, not so much.

Her mental hang ups with men started early in life, when she was a victim of child rape. As a teenager, while strapped to her bed in a mental hospital, she was sexually assaulted almost daily by orderlies. As an adult she used sex as a means to get close enough to kill the world's most dangerous men.

These issues, and others, cause her to hold back.

And that's putting it mildly.

When having sex with me, Callie becomes catatonic.

She'll let me touch her, but when I do her body becomes one giant muscle. Tense, taut, eyes squeezed shut, a grimace on her face. She's got a world-class face and body, but she gives off a vibe like she's being molested. The first time we did it I asked if she was in pain. Then I asked if everything was okay. "Why wouldn't it be?" she said. "We're making love."

But it didn't feel like we were.

Afterward, when I was done, she continued to lie there, as if she thought I was still on top of her. When I pointed out it was over, she said, "I loved it! Thank you!"

The second time we made love it was more of the same. I decided not to tell her I was finished. I climbed off her and watched her face. She continued wincing for more than five minutes before realizing it was over.

"How long have you been finished?" she said, genuinely curious.

"Five minutes."

"Could you do me a favor next time?"

"Name it."

"Could you tap out when you're done?"

"Excuse me?"

"You know, like in MMA, when the guy getting beat taps out? It means he's had enough. Time to quit. Just tap my shoulder."

"Uh...okay."

Like I said, I've got no complaints because I love her. And I understand it's a process.

This time it starts amazingly. She's touching me in such a way that...well, I don't want you to think I've got Kathleen on the brain, but if I didn't know better, I'd swear Kathleen was doing the touching. But as I start to reciprocate, she slowly starts to go stiff, and before long I have to work around her pained expression, lack of warmth, passion, and movement.

My mind drifts to the bathroom encounter I had with Faith Stallone. Faith was a total bitch, but she moved like a woman possessed. Vertically, she was an iceberg. But bend her over a sink and you've got a totally different animal. And I do mean animal! That woman had fire in her panties!

I'm fucking Callie, thinking of Faith. Don't misunderstand: I have zero interest in Faith, but I'm picturing her. It's....

It's a guy thing.

When I'm done, I open my eyes, tap out. Callie shakes her head, as if coming out of a trance. "Better?" she says, hopefully.

"You were amazing!" I say.

"Was it the best sex you ever had?"

"I think it was," I say, lying through my teeth.

"I *told* you!" she said. "And I'm going to keep getting better and better."

That shouldn't be difficult, I think.

We're semi-asleep in each other's arms. As long as I'm not touching her in a sexual way, she's as warm and playful as a puppy. I sleep a little, wake a little, breathing in her scent. There's no place on earth I'd rather be.

Shortly after 1:00 a.m., Vegas time, my phone rings.

Sherm Phillips, Secretary of Defense.

I put him on speaker.

"What's up, Sherm?"

"Ryan Decker."

"What about him?"

"He struck."

I rise to a sitting position. "How bad is it?"

"It could be worse."

"Tell me."

"He wiped out a small neighborhood."

"How small?"

"Eight houses, they think."

"Where?"

"Louisville, Kentucky."

"Any casualties?"

"Yes."

"Shit. How many?"

"We're working on it. When can you get there?"

"Four hours, give or take."

"Let me know what you find."

I hang up, turn toward Callie.

She's gone!

She was here a few seconds ago, now she's gone. Yes, I was concentrating on the call, but I never saw her move, and never felt it.

She's a true ninja.

I hear the toilet flush, the shower turn on.

That's Callie.

She'll be ready to roll inside ten minutes. And that includes packing.

What a helluva woman she is!

Chapter 4

Maybe Taylor.

MAYBE'S BEEN COOLING her heels in Milo's basement for three hours. Lemon's been home half that time. She showered first, then started making dinner.

It's dark before Jake rings the doorbell.

Three wireless pinhole cameras record the events taking place upstairs. Areas of coverage include the kitchen, dining room, and den.

Maybe's monitoring everything on her cell phone.

She didn't bother placing a camera in the bedroom, because when a woman cooks dinner for her lover, the natural progression is kitchen, dining room, den, bedroom.

And they won't make it past the den.

Maybe's first thought was kill them quickly and get it over with. But she finds the whole Lemon-Jake dynamic interesting, and whatever Lemon's preparing—some sort of pasta with grilled chicken, spinach, smoked bacon, and pine nuts—smells divine. Also, Maybe has no close friends, and rarely gets to enjoy an evening out. She hopes to mix business and pleasure this time.

Lemon fusses over the food for another 15 minutes before lighting the candles and placing dinner on the table.

When the lovers take their seats, Maybe climbs the stairs.

Chapter 5

MAYBE GOES STRAIGHT to the kitchen, picks up a plate, helps herself to some pasta, and enters the dining room saying, "Please. Don't get up. Let's enjoy this wonderful dish."

Of course, Lemon screams.

Of course, Jake jumps to his feet.

Now Lemon's standing, too.

For a moment, they're frightened. But Jake's a big guy, in his thirties, and Maybe's practically a child, in comparison. He erroneously comes to the conclusion she's not a serious threat. He's cursing, shouting, making rude comments.

This is how it is for Maybe, the girl with no friends. Is it really asking so much for people to share a simple dinner with her? Obviously yes, since Jake's coming around the table in a huff, saying something about how he's going to throw her ass out.

Maybe opens her jacket, points to the .380 holstered under her arm.

"You like this?" she says, addressing Lemon. "It's a tank top with a built-in holster. Fits snug against the side of my boob. Completely undetectable when I'm wearing a light jacket."

Jake hesitates, then wishes he hadn't.

Not that it matters. She could kick both their asses, even if they had knives.

Which they don't.

She lifts the Velcro safety strap, removes the gun, points it at Jake.

"Have a seat, tough guy."

Jake and Lemon look at each other.

Maybe adds, "Before you decide to go Rambo, think about your friends, Lexi and Byron. I know the cops like Byron's ex-wife for the murders, but that's my handiwork, not hers."

Lemon goes from worried to terrified. Jake isn't so sure. He eyes her carefully. Could this be some sort of prank? If so, he doesn't want to come across like a pussy.

Maybe understands the developing dynamic, and wonders if she should just kill them now if they're not going to have a pleasant dinner together. She ratchets a round into the chamber, and Jake finally gets it.

He moves toward Lemon.

Poor Lemon. It's all moving way too fast for her. Tears are streaming down her cheeks, but she hasn't thought to start crying yet. Her body's reacting to the stress, but in a manner that's completely out of synch. She's shivering and shuddering, and probably doesn't even realize it. "Wh-what do you *want?*" she says.

"For starters, I'd like you both to sit down. Then I'd like us to have a nice dinner, and maybe some light conversation."

"If this is about the lottery money," Jake says...

"It's not. Please sit. I'm making an effort to be friendly. But if you're not interested, I'm prepared to shoot you where you stand."

They look at each other again, then sit.

Maybe places her gun on the table, spears some pasta with her fork, and takes a bite. "Omigod!" she says. "Lemon, you've outdone yourself. You simply *must* give me the recipe."

It takes a few minutes before Lemon and Jake realize they're expected to eat. When they finally start, it's obvious they're not enjoying the food.

"This always happens," Maybe says. "I fear I'm incapable of making friends."

She takes a moment to glance at the latest text message from Milo, who's had a change of heart and wants her to spare Lemon's life. Says he understands he still has to pay her the hundred grand. Hopes she gets the message in time.

Maybe can claim it either way, and decides to let Lemon make the decision.

When their dinner conversation grinds to a complete stop, Maybe motions them to the den, has them sit together on the couch. Claims the comfy chair for herself. Lemon's trembling like a Teacup Maltese getting a shot at the vet's office. Jake holds her hand. Maybe stares at them a moment.

"Please," Lemon says. "Don't do this. You can have anything you want."

"Good to know. What I'd like is for you to tell me what's going on here, and why."

Maybe's attitude hits Jake the wrong way. He's suddenly less frightened, less concerned for his personal safety. Perhaps he's not convinced she has the guts to pull the trigger. Or maybe in his mind this has gone far enough. After all, Jake's a full-grown man, and though Maybe's athletic, she's small, and barely 20 years old. He probably visualizes lunging at her, grabbing the gun, smacking the shit out of her. Visualizes himself standing over her, strong, powerful, in control. Visualizes her on the floor, sobbing, begging his forgiveness while he lectures her about pointing a loaded gun at people.

Jake makes his voice as big and powerful as possible and says, "What's going on here is none of your business, bitch."

Lemon catches the slight change in Maybe's expression, and gives Jake a frightened warning look. She says, "Jake and I are good friends. Nothing more."

Maybe says, "Lemon, you're adorable. I totally get why a loser like Jake would put his marriage on the line. You're a helluva catch. What I don't understand is what you see in him. He's a pig."

"I—"

"Yes?"

"I love him...You know, as a friend."

Maybe leans forward, casually reaches under her chair, produces a handgun complete with silencer. She notes a definite change in their expressions as they come to the realization her visit wasn't spur-of-the-moment. It suddenly dawns on them she's been here a long time. Long enough to hide a gun under the chair before Lemon came home.

When their eyes are large enough to show they understand the implications, Maybe says, "They know."

"I-I beg your pardon?" Lemon says.

"Milo and Faith. They know all about your affair."

"There's no affair," Jake says. "This is two people, two *friends*, having dinner together. Nothing else."

With a flick of her wrist, Maybe points the gun at Jake and puts a bullet between his eyes.

Lemon freaks out.

Vomits.

Pisses.

Screams.

Throws herself on Jake's dead body.

Screams some more.

Maybe says, "I know you're upset, but I like you. If you quiet down, I'll let you live."

Lemon—bless her heart—looks up in disbelief, and makes the world's most valiant attempt to calm herself. It takes 20 seconds to stop crying, and another 20 to stop huffing.

"Thank you!" she says. "Thank you for letting me live."

"You're welcome. And thanks for being calm. There's something very likeable about you. Under different circumstances, I bet we could be friends."

"Th-thank you."

She hiccups.

Maybe arches an eyebrow. Then says, "I don't like what you did with Jake."

"I know how it looks—hic! But we're just friends—hic!—I swear."

Maybe sighs. "That's not true, Lemon."

"I love my husband." —Hic!

"You know what I hate worse than a liar? Nonstop hiccupping."

"I'm sorry." –Hic! "But Jake and I weren't having an affair, his *wife* was!" –Hic! "She had sex with a stranger in the men's room of a bar!"

"*Tattletale!*" Maybe shouts.

"I–I..." —Hic!

"You've got a lot to say about *Faith*, don't you!"

"W-Well—"

"Tell me about the toothbrush."

—Hic!— "Th-the...*what?*" —Hic!

"Milo's toothbrush."

"I don't know what you're—"

"Did you stuff Milo's toothbrush up Jake's ass?"

—Hic!— "*What?*"

Maybe goes quiet.

....Hic!

Lemon feels she should say something, but everything she's said so far seems to be working against her.

....Hic!

The two women stare at each other.

....Hic!

Maybe says, "As stuffy as Milo is, I think the toothbrush thing is sort of funny. I'm not happy you've been cheating on him, and even less happy you keep lying to me about it. But Milo's a weasel. I like you better."

"Th-Thank you." —Hic!—

"Your taste in men sucks."

Lemon nods. —Hic!—

As bad as Milo is, you managed to find someone even worse. I mean, *Jake?* Jesus, Lemon! You should thank me for saving you a lifetime of misery."

"Th-Thank you." —Hic!—

"God, that's annoying. You really need to stop that shit."

—Hic!—

Maybe frowns. "I'll make you a deal: If you can stop hiccupping for five minutes, I'll let you live."

—Hic!—

Maybe laughs. "I won't count that one." She checks her watch. "Starting now."

—Hic!—

Lemon sees the barrel turning toward her face and wonders if Maybe plans to let that one slide, also.

She doesn't.

After firing her weapon, Maybe remains seated, while contemplating the differences in human bone structure. While Jake's head is perfectly intact, Lemon's is all over the place.

Go figure.

She heads to the kitchen, helps herself to some more pasta. While eating, she spies the recipe card on the counter, silently thanks Lemon for providing it, and stuffs it in her pocket.

Home invasions don't require much staging.

Maybe washes her dinner plate, collects the shell casings and pinhole cameras, wipes her prints from whatever she touched during the time her gloves were off. She gives the place a once-over and heads to the back door. As she opens it, the house blows up.

Maybe's disoriented, but smart enough to dive to the floor. She rolls under the large chunk of kitchen counter that's now in the rear entry way. It takes her a few seconds to realize the blast came from the front of the house.

Which is the only reason she's still alive.

She hears additional blasts all around her, as if someone's bombing the neighborhood.

Is it safe to run out the back door?

Another blast rocks the house.

Safe or not, it's time to make tracks!

Maybe scrambles to her feet, tries to run out the door, but the third blast causes the back of the house to come crashing down on her.

Chapter 6

Ryan Decker.

DECKER WATCHES HIS men blow up the neighborhood with bazookas.

Well, shoulder-launched, rocket-propelled missiles, to be exact.

The term "bazooka" hasn't been used by the Army since the 1960's, but try telling that to civilians. If Decker's monkeys want to call them bazookas, who gives a shit?

To be honest, Decker thought there'd be more damage. Each round from this distance is equivalent to a stick of dynamite. He knows these are nicer-than-average houses, but his men have each fired three missiles, and most of the homes are still standing.

He sighs. These guys are thugs, not military, and this is their first real-life attempt with RPG's.

It shows.

Speaking into his mouthpiece, he orders them to fire two more rounds, and challenges them to level the structures. They give it their best, and though it takes nearly twice as many rounds as Decker thought necessary, five gets the job done.

He says, "Gunners, shoot any survivors you see. Then plant your BWC flags, and get the hell out of there!"

A minute later, the soft hum of a dozen electric bikes fill the air. They only cover 25 miles at 20 miles per hour on a single charge, but the furthest residence was only a half-mile from the trucks. The men drive the bikes up the ramps and into the semi's. Once in, they angle the bikes into braces and tie them in place with bungee cords. By then the foot soldiers—the gunners—have returned. They place their weapons in the truck, push the ramps into their slots, climb in the back, close the doors, and knock on the wall to let the drivers know it's time to roll.

Decker, riding shotgun in the first truck, checks his watch. The entire attack took nine minutes.

He frowns.

"I hope the others did better than we did."

Chapter 7

Donovan Creed.

AS CALLIE AND I cross the tarmac, heading to our private jet, Sherm calls to say Decker's men hit another small neighborhood in Jackson, Mississippi.

"Any witnesses?"

"No ground reports yet. Check out Jackson first, then Louisville. And Creed?"

"Yeah?"

"Before you say 'I told you so,' it's still not worth a billion dollars."

"I agree. But after this I'll kill him before letting you pay him a cent."

"That's the spirit. But I think when people hear about this, the singing will start."

"What singing?"

"Decker's women. It's one thing to write on people's asses in the park. But you can't tell me a hundred American women are gonna stand for *this* bullshit."

Sherm's right.

By the time we land in Jackson, more than fifty of Decker's college-aged men and women have come forward to tell authorities what they know.

Unfortunately, they know very little about Decker, and nothing about the bombing.

The geeks know plenty about the bombing, though, and call to brief me. They're skilled at telling me exactly what I need to hear in the briefest manner possible. When they've finished updating me, I pass the information on to Callie.

"Eight homes in Louisville," I say, "And eight more in Jackson."

"Any idea why he chose these two neighborhoods?"

"Both were good targets: small, exclusive, with multi-million dollar homes. Neither were gated. Both neighborhoods had homes situated along a circle, with a common entrance and exit."

"That must fit a thousand locations across the country."

"I agree."

"Why wealthy homes?" she asks.

"Intimidation. Better news coverage."

"Why these two cities?"

"I don't know. But that's something the FBI can follow up on. They can run a check on all the homeowners and their relatives, and try to establish a common connection."

"Think there *is* one?"

"No. But it's worth checking."

"What's the body count?"

"They're still searching the rubble. But so far we're 15 Louisville, 18 Jackson."

"Any owners decide *not* to come home tonight?"

"That's a damn good question. Remind me to ask the police when we get there."

By the time we get to the blast site the Jackson body count is complete at 21, with no survivors.

The bomb squad spokesman tells us the attackers used shoulder-fired missiles, probably RPG-7's.

I call Joe Penny and repeat what I've been told. He says, "That's one of the least-efficient ways to bring down a house."

"Why?"

"Those types of rounds were designed as antitank weapons."

"So?"

"It'd be hard to contain the shells inside a normal home. They're just as likely to blast right through the front and back of the house and blow up in the yard. See any evidence of that?"

"No. These homes are decimated."

Joe pauses a moment. Then says, "Foreign surplus, delayed fuse."

"Excuse me?"

"Their rocket launchers must've had diminished propulsion capabilities, with missiles wired to blow up seconds after impact."

"I have no idea what you're talking about."

"Shoulder-launchers are anti-tank weapons. Current U.S. rocket launchers are too powerful to use on civilian homes."

"What's your best guess?"

"Decker must have bought some older RPG's and modified them."

"Why do that?"

"Harder to trace the sale of that many RPG's."

"Unless we can find out what country sold them to him."

"That won't happen. RPG's are used by the armies of 40 different countries and dozens of terrorist organizations. So it could be an army, ex-army, terrorists, or militia groups."

"In other words, they're untraceable."

"That's my guess," Joe says.

Chapter 8

I HAVE TO give serious props to the police, National Guard, and local builders, who have assembled an amazing array of industrial lighting equipment, powered by massive generators. Giant floodlights hang from six moveable cranes, illuminating the fourth house on the block as if it were mid-day. The cranes will stay in place till the operators receive the go-ahead to move to the fifth house. All houses were previously searched for bodies and survivors, and now the explosives experts are taking photos and combing through the rubble to piece together any information that might prove beneficial later on.

"No survivors?" I ask the lead investigator.

"Thought we had one, but he died in the ambulance."

"Did he say anything?"

"Nope. We found him unconscious, he died the same way."

Decker's men planted a flag in each yard after the attacks. White, with red lettering: *BWC.*

The lead guy sees Callie staring at the flag. "Don't touch that," he says. "We haven't had time to dust it for prints yet."

Callie gives him a withering look.

He says, "Sorry. I know it's not your first rodeo."

"So I can't blow my nose into it?" she says.

With no survivors or witnesses to interview, Callie and I are beyond frustrated. We're decent fire investigators, but this type of rubble-sifting is beyond our expertise. I mean, had we been first on the scene, she and I could have looked at the damage and determined how the attack took place, and the approximate locations from which the weapons had been fired. But the munitions experts already made those determinations prior to our arrival.

My phone vibrates. "Text from Curly," I say.

Callie says, "No more attacks, I hope."

"Louisville had four survivors."

"That's good news. Has anyone made a statement?"

"No. All four are in critical condition."

"I bet at least one will pull through."

"Let's move on," I say. "There's nothing for us to do here."

A few minutes later, while talking to the limo driver, I notice Callie has turned her back to me. Her handbag's on her shoulder, but it's in front of her, not at her side. And her head's tilted, as if she's looking at something in front of her.

Like her cell phone.

"Everything all right?" I call out.

She turns her head. "Nothing I can't handle."

I can't see what she's doing, but I know she's sending a text message.

I'm not a jealous guy.

Suspicious, yes.

Moments later, in the car, I notice Callie's stone-faced, staring straight ahead as if the weight of the world is on her shoulders.

I ask, "Is there something I should know?"

"Yes."

"Tell me."

"I love you."

"Anything else?"

"Nope, that's it."

"Am I allowed to ask about the person you just texted?"

"No."

I wait, but she says nothing.

"I'm trying to trust you," I say.

"I'm trying to be trustworthy."

I study her expression, but Callie gives up very little.

Chapter 9

Callie Carpenter.

DECKER'S UPPED THE ante. In the space of minutes, he went from ass-writing to murder. While it's exactly what Callie anticipated, she now finds herself in a sticky situation.

Moments ago, Decker texted: "*We've got a serious problem.*"

Callie texted: "*I've upheld my end.*"

"*I know. But something horrible happened. Tell me if this is who I think it is.*"

She opens the attachment.

It's a photo of Kimberly Creed, a.k.a. Maybe Taylor.

"WTF?" Callie writes.

Decker writes, "*Is it her?*"

"*Yes. Is she dead?*"

"*No. But she's critical.*"

Chapter 10

NOW, BACK IN the car, she feels Creed staring at her. He saw her texting, and knows something's up. He's talking about wanting to trust her.

She says, "I'm not cheating on you."

He says, "I believe you. But you're upset."

"Actually, I'm feeling sick to my stomach. Can you ask the driver to pull over?"

He does, and Callie jumps out. When Creed starts to follow, she says, "Please wait for me in the car. I don't want you to see me this way."

His look says he saw her palm her phone.

Doesn't matter. This is more important than any argument they could possibly have. She texts, *"How did this happen?"*

"I don't know. She got in the line of fire somehow."

"You better hope she survives."

"*I can't let that happen. I have to kill her.*"

Callie texts: "*If you spare her, I'll protect you.*"

"*Explain.*"

"*I won't let Creed kill you.*"

"*He'll kill me anyway. For letting this happen.*"

"*If you protect Kimberly, I'll protect you.*"

He pauses a moment, then texts: "*How much trouble am I in?*"

Callie: "*You don't want to know.*"

Decker: "*I'll spare her on one condition. Kill Jack Tallow.*"

"*Why?*"

"*Can't say. That's the deal. Take it or leave it.*"

"*I'll take it. Where is he?*"

"*If I knew that, I'd kill him myself.*"

"*I'll find and eliminate him.*"

"*I want your word you won't interrogate him first.*"

"*You have my word. And my advice: If Kimberly dies, kill yourself.*"

"*Understood.*"

Callie breathes a sigh of relief, climbs back in the car.

Creed says, "You didn't bother to fake being sick just now."

"No. But everything's okay."

"Sorry, but it's not."

She looks at him. "I thought you trusted me."

"I thought I did, too."

She looks out the window a minute, then says, "Can we pretend the texting didn't happen just now?"

"No."

She starts to say something, then changes her mind. "Suit yourself," she says.

They ride to the jet in heavy silence. When they pass the gates to enter the private airfield, Callie says, "I know we're not speaking at the moment, but can I ask you a question?"

"Of course."

"Where's Jack Tallow?"

"New Orleans.

"Rose Dumont Hotel?"

He nods.

"And the babe?"

"Jill?"

"Yeah. Where is *she*?"

"Someplace safe. Till her husband's out of the picture."

"Someplace *safe*? You won't tell me where?"

"It's more like I'm wondering why you care."

"She's in this thing somehow."

"I doubt that. She gave us the sketch."

"Are you sure it's accurate? I mean, how many positive hits have you gotten from it?"

"Do you have anything substantial, or is this about your jealousy issues?"

"It's a feeling."

"Women's intuition?"

Callie gives him an angry look. "Assassin's intuition." — and catches herself before adding, *Like you used to have, before you started fucking Kathleen again.*

He says, "I think Jill will be safer if I keep her location a secret."

"So much for trust," she says.

The limo comes to a stop a few yards from the jet.

Creed says, "Jack's at the hotel, convalescing. He's being treated by one of our company physicians. He's staying under an assumed name."

"That's very chatty of you to say."

"I'm comfortable telling you all that because I can assure you he has no idea where Jill is."

"And you think I'm planning to kill Jill."

"Honestly? I have no idea what you might be up to."

She nods. "Thanks for the trust."

"Don't mention it."

"I thought I was the jealous one."

"You are. It's unhealthy how jealous you are."

They stare into each other's eyes. Neither blinks.

Callie says, "How jealous do you think I am?"

"I'm not sure. But lately I find myself wondering if you're jealous enough to kill Kathleen and leave her daughter an orphan."

"That's a lovely sentiment to express about the woman you're supposed to love."

They continue staring without blinking. Somehow, without a word being said, they're in a blinking competition.

Five minutes later Creed says, "I can keep this up all night."

"Then why don't you?"

"Because we've got witnesses to interview in Louisville. If you like, we can move this staring contest to the jet."

"I'm not going with you."

He looks at her with genuine surprise. "The person you're texting wins out?"

She shrugs. "I can't be with a man who doesn't trust me."

They stare at each other until he says, "Do you still work for me?"

She thinks about it a minute, still not blinking. Then says, "I don't know. It's up to you."

"The person who texted you. Man or woman?"

"Does it matter?"

"I suppose not."

"See you around," she says.

"Whatever," he says.

They continue staring.

After a while, Creed says, "What's the longest you've ever gone without blinking?"

"Two days. You?"

"Two days."

"Figures."

He says, "I have to go to Louisville."

"So go."

"I will. But just so you know, I won't be blinking for the next three days."

"Who gives a shit?"

"You do."

She says, "Honor system?"

"Fine. Text me when you blink."

"I'll blink after you text me that you blinked."

"What're we, eight years old?"

"More like eight-year mental patients."

He says, "Did we just break up?"

"Probably."

"How long would we have gone without killing each other?"

Callie says, "I could kill you this very second."

"I seriously doubt that."

She wiggles the fingers of her right hand. From out of thin air, a knife has appeared.

Without moving his eyes from hers, he says, "I saw you go for the knife."

"If you had, you would've gone for yours."

He wiggles the fingers of *his* right hand.

She says, "Nicely done."

"Thanks."

She says, "If you ever need to talk?"

"Yeah?"

"Call me."

"You too."

They exit the limo from opposite doors and back away from each other without taking their eyes off each other's faces. He backs up across the tarmac toward the jet's staircase, reaches behind him for the railing, finds it, and climbs backwards up the steps. She walks backwards all the way to the door of the private aviation terminal.

Once inside, she charters a flight to New Orleans.

Chapter 11

Faith Stallone.

"ARE YOU REALLY that stupid?" Faith asks. "It would look suspicious if we *didn't* call each other! She blew up the whole fucking neighborhood!"

"No she didn't," Milo says. "Turn on your TV. It's that crazy urban terrorist group that wrote on people's asses in Central Park."

"You don't think your hit woman killed our spouses and blew up the neighborhood to pin the blame on Ryan Decker?"

"No. I think it's a coincidence."

"That would be a hell of a coincidence."

"It's only a coincidence from our standpoint. Yours and mine. Not the world's."

"What are you trying to say?"

"Every day hundreds of people get murdered. And every now and then, bombs blow up somewhere. But these are two separate events. We hired a hit woman, and Decker blew up two neighborhoods. One of the neighborhoods happened to be mine, which is the only thing that makes it a coincidence. But that's *our* coincidence, not the world's. So if you still think Maybe Taylor did it, how do you explain the neighborhood that got blown up in Jackson, Mississippi?"

"I can't. But either way, we're in a world of shit."

"Don't fall apart on me, Faith. Are you still at your sister's?"

"Yes. And you're in South Carolina."

"As planned. When's the last time you heard from Jake?"

"A few hours before he and Lemon were killed in your house."

"If Jake's dead, she probably killed him at *your* house."

"Then how did she get caught in your neighborhood?"

"What are you *talking* about?"

Who's called you so far?"

"About a dozen people."

"I mean, which of our friends?"

"There seem to be fewer and fewer of them. But the ones we hang out with have called to touch base. Brody sent me pictures of what's left of the house."

"You don't sound very upset over losing it."

"Are you kidding? It's the best thing that could've happened! It's been a fucking money pit! I'm mortgaged to my eyeballs. Thank God for insurance."

244

"If they pay."

"Of course they'll pay!"

"On TV they said some homeowner's policies won't pay for acts of terrorism."

"*What?*"

"Better check your coverage."

"Oh, wouldn't *that* be the icing on the cake."

"Let's focus on Jake and Lemon. Why do you think they were at my house?"

"I think Jake was there. Without Lemon."

"Why?"

"Lemon called me last night to say she was spending the night at our lake house."

"It was an excuse, you moron."

"I don't think so. I backed out. I told Maybe Taylor not to kill Lemon."

"You're joking, right?"

"I couldn't go through with it. I said if she spared Lemon, I'd pay her fee."

"She shafted you, Milo. Lemon's dead."

"No. I would have heard."

"If Lemon was alive, she would have called you by now. Her *house* has been blown up!"

"I doubt she's heard about it. We don't have TV or Internet service at the lake house, and she can't get telephone coverage unless she's standing at the top of the driveway."

"She didn't go to the lake house, Milo. That was an excuse. She didn't want you checking up on her. Go online.

Read the latest updates. Jake and Lemon are dead. Check the Internet."

"I did. They haven't released any names."

"True. But an FBI spokesman said a man and woman had been found in one of the houses. They'd been shot in the head at point blank range prior to the attack. If that's not Lemon and Jake, that *would* be the biggest coincidence in history! They also said a woman was found with shell casings and surveillance equipment in her pocket. If that's not Maybe Taylor, I'll eat your car."

She waits for him to say something. When he doesn't, she says, "Are you listening to me? We've got a problem. They captured Maybe Taylor. If she talks, we're fucked."

"Lemon's dead?"

"Yeah. She's dead, asshole. Thanks to you and your crazy-ass hit woman. And thanks to you, we're in deep shit. So you need to get your ass back to town. I can't believe you did this to us! I will *never* forgive you." She pauses. "Are you listening to me?"

"I can't believe she killed Lemon after I asked her not to."

"Did you talk to her in person?"

"No. I texted her."

"If the police have her phone—"

"I wish you hadn't said that. You know what I think?"

"No. And I don't care."

"I think we should hire another hit person to kill Maybe Taylor."

Faith thinks about it a minute. "That's the first intelligent thing you've said since this whole thing started. Do you know someone?"

"I can ask my client."

"No. That would be stupid. There can't be a whole lot of hit men running around. Maybe probably knows the same people your client knows."

"I could call Sal Bonadello."

"The crime boss?"

"Uh huh."

"You know him?"

"Nope. But I'm willing to meet him, if you're willing to pay."

"I'm willing to discuss it. In the meantime, contact him, see what he says."

"Okay."

Chapter 12

Donovan Creed.

I'M NOT SURE what Callie's going through right now, but it's so typically Callie, the way she's shutting down. I've seen it many times over the years, so I don't know why I thought things would be different just because she's dating me.

What was it she said in Jackson? "Can we pretend the texting didn't happen just now?"

Wouldn't *that* be a crazy way to live? Every time she does something wrong we can just pretend it never happened.

I wonder what she's up to.

I don't think it involves Jack Tallow, or Jill DiPiese. But this thing she said about Jill has me thinking. What if Jill's been in contact with Decker? What if she gave us a phony description?

Jack Tallow vouched for it, but what do we really know about him? He supposedly met Decker years ago. But was he covering for Jill? I'd like to think not, as angry as he seemed to be with her in the limo.

When my jet touches down in Louisville, I notice a car waiting beside the limo I ordered. I descend the steps and meet FBI Special Agent Brad Dung.

"Odd name," I say.

"What, Donovan Creed? I agree. I bet the other kids used to give you hell about it."

"Ah. A G-man with a sense of humor."

"My bureau apparently has a bigger one. We spent hours culling information from the blast site."

"So?"

"They ordered me to share it with you."

"The FBI's sharing data? Did I just land in Opposite Land?"

"Apparently, because nothing makes sense."

"Wait," I say. "I get it. You guys are about to get slammed by the media for letting this happen. You've had three chances to catch the guy, three chances to prevent Louisville and Jackson from being bombed."

"Your point?"

"By sharing data with Homeland Security, your bosses are shifting half the burden to our department. From now on we'll both look like we've got our heads up our asses."

"You might be right. Can I ask you something?"

"Go ahead."

"Have you recently had a face lift?"

"No. Why do you ask?"

"You're not blinking your eyes. Why not?"

"It shows weakness."

"You people are fucked."

I glance at his government-issue car and say, "Why don't you park that piece of shit and ride to the site with me in style?"

"That'll work. Except we're not going to the site."

"Why not?"

"They want you at Mercy Hospital."

"Someone's conscious?"

"Not yet. But we've got some interesting situations developing."

"Like what?"

"I'll tell you in the car."

Chapter 13

"DOES THE NAME Milo Fister mean anything to you?" Agent Dung asks. "He's an attorney, here in Louisville."

He hands me a grainy photo, obviously pulled from the Internet.

I shake my head.

"What about his wife, Lemon Fister? Up-and-coming socialite?"

"That's a name I'd remember. What, no photo?"

"Working on it."

"Did they survive?"

"We don't think so."

"Either they did or they didn't."

"We're literally moments away from having a positive ID."

"Good. What makes this couple so special?"

"They were executed before the attack."

"By 'executed,' you mean what, exactly?"

"They each took a bullet to the head. Between the eyes."

I frown.

"There's more," he says. "A young woman was found in the same house, near the back door. She was badly hurt in the explosion, but she's alive."

"Got a name on that one?"

"Yeah. Jane Doe." He laughs. "But we think she's the shooter."

"Why?"

"Police recovered two shells in her pocket, and three pinhole cameras."

"The footage she took is probably on her cell phone."

"We think so too. But it's encrypted."

"Your guys can crack that."

"Sure. Eventually. But there's a government footprint on the encryption." He notes my blank look and adds, "A marker. Her phone is protected by some sort of government encryption."

I'm rapidly developing a sick feeling in my stomach. "What's her condition?"

"She'll live."

There aren't many female assassins in the country, and I make it my business to know them all. But this one sounds like my daughter, Kimberly, who goes by the name Maybe Taylor.

"Got a picture of the shooter?" I say.

"Thought you'd never ask."

He turns his cell phone toward me, shows me a picture of Kimberly.

My heart skips a beat, but I can't let my expression show recognition. In the photo, she looks dead. Thank God Agent Dung already said she's going to live. I'll have to trust him on that. In the meantime, I need to get the focus off Kimberly. They're already building a murder case against her, and have obviously sent this photo to police and FBI all over the country. It might very well be on the evening news tonight. If it is, she'll be identified.

I ask, "Was Milo a criminal attorney?"

"Predominantly, yes."

"Sounds like a gangland murder."

"We agree. But we can't figure out how it ties into Decker blowing up the neighborhood."

"When we get to the hospital, any chance I can have a few minutes alone with her?"

"Not officially."

"But...?"

"We realize you have more latitude than we do in these situations. The government actually cares if *we* break laws."

"Right. And when you guys retire, no one shows up to kill you."

"There's that."

"I assume they're considering Jane Doe a murder suspect, and not one of the bombers?"

"That's right, and that's the problem. The bombers haven't officially been classified as terrorists. But if that changes, I'm told you have the power to classify her as a possible terrorist, which would allow you to interrogate her. Is that a fair assessment of how your department operates?"

"Off the record?"

"Of course."

"It is. But not in high-visibility cases like this one."

"I really want to find out what she knows," Dung says. "After the police do their thing I'm willing to create a diversion to buy you some time with her."

"I'd appreciate that."

"Two stipulations."

"Name them."

"She'll have to survive your interview."

"You have my word. What's the second thing?"

"You'll have to record the interview and let us make a copy."

"No problem."

When we arrive at the hospital I tell Agent Dung I need to make a couple of quick calls to let Homeland Security know about the upcoming interview. He tells me where to meet him when I'm finished.

I use the time to make five calls.

Callie doesn't answer.

Nat Flemming does.

"Nat, it's Donovan Creed."

"Holy shit!"

"Ready for the big leagues?"

"I've been waiting two years for this call. Where and when?"

"For now I just need a warning shot. When can you be in place?"

"Zone 1?"

"Yes."

"Twenty minutes, give or take."

"Good man."

Third call is to Layla Hart. When she answers, I say, "It's Donovan Creed. You're being activated."

"Thank you, sir! When do I start?"

"Immediately."

"Not to sound mercenary, but how will this affect my pay?"

"That's your second question?"

"I'm sort of dating a guy. It's gotten serious."

"I'd have to check what starting salary is these days. But activation bonus is a million."

"Wow! Can I keep the guy?"

"Have we vetted him?"

"Not officially."

"If he passes you can date him between assignments. But you can't tell him anything about your work."

"Of course. Where do you need me?"

"Florida."

"When?"

"Instantly. Pack your things. C.H. will call you with details."

"What does C.H. stand for?"

"I honestly don't know. But you'll know him by his voice."

"Why's that?"

"He's an elf."

She pauses. "This is a test, right? *Shit!* I know this. It's a clandestine group or a code name for someone."

"Relax. It's neither. C.H. is an actual woodland elf."

"There's no such thing."

"Don't tell C.H."

Fourth call is to C.H. the elf. I tell him what I need.

"I'll take care of it," he says.

I hang up, take a deep breath, and make the fifth call.

Chapter 14

"HELLO?"

"Janet, it's me."

"What do *you* want?"

"I need a favor."

"Fuck you!"

"This is important."

"Your favors ended with the divorce papers."

"It's about Kimberly."

"What about her?"

"I need you to take her shopping today."

"What are you *talking* about? Kimberly's in Las Vegas."

"She's on her way to your place. She'll be there in two hours. She'll stay with you a few days. It'll be like old times. Except not exactly. When she gets her luggage situated, you'll take her shopping. You'll buy something nice for yourself on her credit card. My treat. A dress, a car—whatever you want. You'll have lunch at a public place, you'll laugh, you'll hug each other like the old days. But make sure the neighbors see you together. And don't be afraid to let her talk to the neighbors."

"Do you have any idea how insane you sound?"

"No."

"I don't know what type of relationship you have with our daughter, but Kimberly always calls before showing up. We make plans."

"When's the last time you heard from her?"

"Yesterday."

"Well, she's been in an accident."

"*What?*"

"You know the bombs that went off in Jackson and Louisville?"

"*You* did that?"

"No, of course not. It was a terrorist attack. Anyway, Kimberly was...visiting one of the homes."

She says nothing, so I add, "At the time of the bombing."

She says, "If she was in an accident, why would she want to go shopping?"

I sigh.

Civilians.

Jesus.

"Look, I know this won't make any sense to you," I say. "But in a few hours Kimberly's photo will be all over the news."

"Why?"

"Two of the bombing victims were shot before the attack."

"What attack?"

"The fucking *bombing* attack. Are you paying attention?"

"What does the bombing attack have to do with Kimberly?"

"The FBI thinks she shot and killed two people. The whole thing's a misunderstanding, and I can fix it. But I can't fix it in time to keep her photo from going out. What I'm saying, I need you to do something for me. For Kimberly, I mean."

"I have no idea what you're talking about. But I can't wait to hear the favor."

"I already told you. I want you to take her shopping today."

The line goes dead.

I call back. "We got disconnected."

"Yeah, we did. Because I hung up on you."

"You knew I'd call you back."

"If you had the time."

I frown. "I'm trying to solve this issue with Kimberly."

"Then tell the fucking truth for once in your life! Our daughter's a school teacher in Las Vegas. It makes no sense she'd be in Louisville, or that the FBI considers her a murder suspect. But if they did, I doubt they'd let her flee the state to go shopping with me. So what the fuck is going on? Where's Kimberly?"

"You mean right now?"

"No. I mean six years ago when I caught you in the lady's room at Starbucks with that Irish whore!"

"She wasn't a whore. She was a CIA agent."

"You were kissing her on the floor!"

"Jesus, Janet. We've been through this a hundred times. The agent was late to our meeting, I found her unconscious in the women's room. I gave her mouth-to-mouth. And—why am I even telling you this?—You weren't even *there*! Your friend, Christine's the one who walked in on us."

"You slept with her."

"You know that's not true. You made me take a polygraph, remember?"

"What sort of spy would you be if you couldn't fake a polygraph?"

I sigh. "Kimberly's in the hospital."

"Bullshit."

"Why are you so difficult to talk to?"

"Because I'm the ex-wife of a pathological liar. Which hospital is she in? I'll call to verify."

"Mercy Hospital, in Louisville. But don't call. And don't tell anyone."

She laughs. "You are so full of shit. Let's see if I've got this right. My daughter's been in a bombing accident in Louisville, Kentucky. She's a patient at Mercy Hospital, but I'm not allowed to call her, or tell anyone. She's a murder suspect, but she's on her way to visit me for a shopping spree."

"I have to tell you something. Don't hang up and don't go nuts on me. This is serious. The woman who's on her way to stay with you is Kimberly's body double. She knows everything there is to know about Kimberly. And looks exactly like her. You wouldn't be able to tell them apart except for the voice. The *real* Kimberly—our daughter—is in the hospital. She'll be fine, but at the moment she's unconscious. They're calling her Jane Doe, and asking the public to identify her. Be we can't let that happen. So when her photo hits the newswires, I don't want your friends and relatives thinking she's Kimberly."

"If you're telling the truth, it *is* Kimberly."

"Yes. But I can't let them identify her."

"They could take her fingerprints."

"She doesn't have fingerprints."

"What are you talking about?"

"I don't have time to get into all that. I'm trying to move her to a safe location."

"She's in the hospital? Swear it. On Kimberly's life."

"I swear."

"You *son of a bitch*! I know you had something to do with this. What's her condition?"

"She's been downgraded to serious."

"*Serious*? What the fuck was it *before*?"

"Critical. But she's doing fine."

"I'm going there. She needs me."

"You can't."

"Don't fucking tell me what I can and can't do! Especially when your solution is for me to go shopping. *Shopping*? Why the fuck would I go *shopping* when my daughter's in the *intensive care unit*?"

"She's been moved out of intensive care—"

I notice an orderly heading toward me, pushing a cart. I give him my full focus in case he's been sent here to assassinate me. As I work out the best way to neutralize him, he passes without incident. I turn my focus back to Janet and say, "Kimberly's in serious danger with the police and FBI, and you're going to have to trust me to solve this. So listen without interrupting. If you don't do *exactly* what I say, I will fucking kill you. You know I'm serious. I'm at Mercy Hospital right now. I've seen Kimberly, and she's going to be fine. The place is crawling with police, detectives, and FBI. I need to get her out of here, and I will, but I can't let them find out who she is. So the body double is going to pose as our daughter, and you're going to play along. And I'll keep you posted on Kimberly's recovery. When everything's safe, you can come to my facility in Virginia and spend as much time with her as you want."

"You wouldn't kill your daughter's mother."

"Hold on, while I conference someone."

I work the buttons on my phone till Nat Flemming says, "I'm here."

"Janet? This is Nat. He works for me."

"Fuck you, Nat," she says.

I ask, "Nat, where's Janet?"

"In the kitchen."

"What the *fuck?*" Janet says.

"Nat, do it!"

He fires a shot through the kitchen window.

Janet screams.

I say, "That was a warning shot to show I'm serious. Nat's going to keep an eye on you till this is over. He's going to pose as Kimberly's boyfriend. Now open the door and let him in, or he'll kill you before you can call 911."

"You're a despicable son of a bitch. A disgusting, whore-mongering, low-life, murderous bastard."

"I agree. And those are the very flaws that kept me from getting a better wife."

"Fuck you!"

Chapter 15

I'M NOT ALONE. There are seven of us standing around Kimberly's hospital bed, waiting for her to regain consciousness. We're told that could happen at any minute, and I'm concerned she'll see me and say something like, "Dad!" that could make it harder for me to get her out of here and have her hospital records erased. If I could be alone with her when she wakes up I could control the situation. But that's not going to happen. I won't be able to meet her privately till the detectives have a chance to try to trick her into saying something they can use against her in court.

As Kimberly's hand twitches, my phone vibrates. On the chance it's Callie, I check it.

"Be right back!" I say to the surprised group.

I leave the room, then click the phone to accept the call from Sal Bonadello, Midwest crime boss.

"What's up, Sal?"

"I heard you're—whatcha call—*cohabitating* with that gorgeous blonde killer that works for you."

"I'm kind of busy right now."

"You're a helluva cocksman, Creed. A *helluva* cocksman! Eight weeks ago you fly here to meet me, end up humpin' a hot MILF in the men's room of a bar. Now Callie Carpenter's dining on Creed steak. How about you—whatcha call—allocate some of that nooky to me?"

"Callie's spoken for."

"I'm talking about the MILF. When a score goes down in my city, I'm supposed to get a taste. And from what I hear, you made a helluva score in the men's room."

"How do you know about that?"

"I hear things."

"Like I said, I'm busy right now. If there's nothing else—"

"You know those guys I told you about eight weeks ago?"

"What about them?"

"They're still alive."

I frown. "Have you been watching the news lately?"

He chuckles. "That Decker's got you runnin' in circles like he's nailed your left foot to the floor."

"I'll thin out your herd when this is over. Anything else?"

"I got a strange phone call just now."

"Can I call you back tonight?"

"Sure, but you'll want to hear this right now."

I sigh. "Please be quick."

"A Louisville attorney asked me to recommend a hit man."

"I hope you gave him someone else."

"Nope. I gave him your name and said you'd call him within 24 hours."

"Why?"

"He wants you to kill one of your people. Maybe Taylor."

I nearly drop my phone.

Sal laughs.

I say, "What's this guy's name?"

"Milo Fister."

I lower my voice to a whisper. "I heard he died."

"You heard wrong. Milo and this other lady hired your daughter to kill their spouses. Now they want to hire someone to kill her. Don't you love it?"

"What's her name?"

"Who, Milo's partner?"

"Yeah."

"Faith Stallone."

"*What?*"

"You've heard of her?"

"The guy Kimberly killed. Was it Jake Stallone?"

"That sounds right. Listen, I want fifty grand for giving you this information."

"Done."

"And pictures of what you do to them. You know how I love pictures."

"We'll see."

Chapter 16

Callie Carpenter.

IT ISN'T HARD for Callie to find Jack Tallow's hotel room. A thousand bucks convinces the concierge she's Jack's sister.

And why shouldn't it?

She knows his real name, knows he's staying at the Rose Dumont under an assumed name, knows the room's being paid by Donovan Creed, knows he's convalescing under a doctor's care, and that the doctor's checking on him every day.

Still, you don't get to be a concierge at the Rose Dumont Hotel by giving out guest information, so the concierge insists on calling Jack personally.

"If he's alone, he'll hiss," Callie says. "He's had an operation, and lost his vocal cords, so tell him to tap the phone once for yes, and twice for no."

"Very well. And your name is?"

"Jill Whittaker."

She calls, Jack taps yes to seeing his sister, Jill Whittaker, and Callie heads to the room. Before knocking, she dons a ball cap, tucks her blonde hair beneath it, turns her collar up and her back to the door. When Jack opens it, she backs inside so quickly and forcefully she knocks him to the floor. She kicks the door shut behind her, jumps over him, comes at him from behind, and pushes a syringe into his neck.

Jack's body goes slack. When he comes to, he finds his arms and legs taped to the desk chair so tightly he can barely wiggle his fingers and toes. His neck is taped to the back of the chair.

She says, "Jack, I want some answers, and I hope you'll be truthful with me. I have numerous ways to encourage your cooperation, and hope the demonstration I'm about to give will prove my point. Tap your right index finger once if you understand."

He does.

"Good. As you can tell, I've taped your neck to the back of the chair. What you probably don't know, I've placed an extension cord around your throat, like a noose, and tied it behind the chair. I worked your toothbrush into the knot, so that by turning the toothbrush clockwise I can tighten the cord around your neck, like so."

She turns the toothbrush till tears form in the corners of Jack's eyes. Then she loosens it, saying, "Everyone I've ever tortured would tell you that was a mild demonstration."

She slides the cord down so it covers his Adam's apple. "I know you've had a brutal neck surgery, and I'll try to respect your healing process. But what type of interrogator would I be if I ignored your wound completely? For this reason, if I think you're lying at any point, I'll crush your Adam's apple. And of course, that will just be a warm up."

He hisses, but not in an angry way.

While cutting part of the tape from Jack's right hand, Callie says, "I'm giving you enough slack to write your answers. I know you can't see what you're writing because of the way I've taped your neck, but I've placed some paper under your hand." She gives him the pen and says, "Is there anything you wish to say before I start?"

He writes: *You're the most beautiful woman I've ever seen.*

"Thank you, Jack. That's nice of you to say."

He adds: *When this is over, would you consider going out with me?*

She laughs. "You've got a winning way about you, Jack. Has anyone ever told you that?"

He writes: *I get that all the time. How about it? Will you go out with me?*

"I'm sort of in a relationship, but sort of not. I guess you could say I'm trying to decide if I'm available."

I'd like to help you make that decision.

"Let's not get ahead of ourselves."

As you wish.

"Have you ever met Ryan Decker in person?"

Yes.

"Thanks for your honesty. Jill DiPiese worked with a sketch artist to produce a drawing of Decker. She gave it to Donovan Creed to disseminate to the media. Is the picture a good likeness?"

No.

Callie does a double-take. "Seriously? Wow. Thanks, Jack. You could have slid that one past me."

What's your name?

Callie.

I will never lie to you, Callie. Why aren't you blinking?

"Personal issue. On a scale of one to ten, with ten being a perfect likeness, how would you rate the drawing Jill released to the media?"

One.

"Why did you tell Creed it was a good likeness?"

I was covering for Jill.

"Why aren't you covering for her now?"

I don't want you to crush my Adam's apple. And I want to go out with you. And I'm faithful.

"Well....thanks. That puts you head and shoulders above the guy I'm currently dating."

Donovan Creed.

"That's right."

Jill stripped for him in the limo.

"Excuse me?"

On the way to New Orleans.

"What do you mean she stripped for him?"

We were stuck in traffic on the interstate. Jill made the others get out of the car. Then she told him she wanted to have sex with him. She said she was sopping wet for him.

Callie's eyes blaze. "You're lying." She moves behind him, reaches for the toothbrush.

Jack slaps the chair.

Callie says, "Why would Jill want to have sex with Creed? He killed her taxi driver friend and slapped her around."

She said she was insanely attracted to dangerous, powerful men.

"When she said she was sopping wet for him what did Creed say?"

He told me to get out of the car.

"Did they have sex?"

I don't know.

"How long were you outside the car?"

Twenty minutes.

Callie bites her lip. Then says, "Did he even mention my name to Jill?"

Jack pauses. Then writes: *Yes. said he was involved with someone.*

"And what did she say?"

She said Callie will never have to know.

"Is it possible you're lying to me?"

I will never lie to you.

"How did you meet Ryan Decker?"

We were planted in the Witness Protection Program together, years ago.

"Planted? By whom?"

A terrorist organization. Now defunct.

"Do you know Decker's real name?"

Yes.

The last person on earth Callie feels like calling is Donovan Creed. But she presses his speed dial key because he needs to hear this. When he answers, she places the phone on the desk beside Jack and says, "You just told me that Jill DiPiese gave Donovan Creed a phony drawing to disseminate to the press, and that Ryan Decker looks nothing like the police artist's sketch. You said you met Ryan Decker when the two of you were planted in the Witness Protection Program together, about two years ago. And you claim to know Decker's real name. Tell me."

Jack writes: *His real name is Austin Rennick. His Witness Protection identity was Chase Bowers.*

Callie relates that message to the phone, then asks, "Jack, do you know what Decker's planning next?"

Yes.

"Tell me."

A swarm.

Chapter 17

Donovan Creed.

THE DOCTORS ARE wrong. Kimberly doesn't come to while we're standing around her bed. In fact, she takes a sudden turn for the worse. A neurologist is summoned, and the doctor makes us leave the room. The detectives post two armed guards outside Kimberly's door.

While waiting for the neurologist, the doctor tells us her spinal cord is fine, and everything from the neck down seems to be in good condition. But they're not sure about her brain injuries. She's sustained some damage, but they can't determine the extent till the neurologist performs some tests. He's telling us this so we'll understand why we can't talk to her anytime soon.

I try not to act too interested. Instead, I ask to meet some of the other survivors. The doc gives me permission to see two of them, and the FBI agents escort me to their rooms.

But it's a waste of time.

Both survivors tell the same story: they went to sleep in their beds and woke up in the hospital.

I call the geeks and tell them to start working on ideas to have Kimberly transferred from Mercy Hospital to Sensory Medical, at my headquarters. Once there, our people can stage her death and give her a new face and identity, same as they did for me a few years back.

Minutes after hanging up, I get a call from Callie.

I'm only mildly surprised to learn she's interrogating Jack Tallow, and reading his written responses so I can hear them. As the call continues it becomes obvious Callie has struck gold.

Chapter 18

Ryan Decker.

RYAN DECKER IS as safe as an American citizen can be.

He entered the Witness Protection Program years ago, received a new name, Chase Bowers, and promptly killed another Witness Protection participant named Ryan Decker, and stole *his* identity.

In other words, the fake Chase Bowers killed the fake Ryan Decker, and stole his identity. Ingenious, because when the Justice Department recently performed an audit of all Witness Protection members only two were missing: Chase Bowers and Luke West.

There may be thousands of Ryan Deckers in the United States, but the one who's bombing neighborhoods is the only Ryan Decker no one's concerned about, because he's in the Witness Protection Program, and has been cleared by the U.S. Marshals' Service.

The second man who disappeared was an acquaintance of Decker's named Luke West, who also killed a Witness Protection participant named Jack Tallow, and assumed *his* identity.

Confusing, but effective.

The "new" Ryan Decker landed a job as a killer drone pilot.

Operating out of Indianapolis, Indiana, Decker flew remote-controlled bombing missions in Afghanistan. He'd sit at his console with a bagel, orange juice, and morning paper, turn on his monitor, fire up his drone, and follow a flight plan designed by the Air Force. He'd eat a bagel, sip some orange juice, press a button, blow up a bunker, house, or bridge.

Because the killing takes place thousands of miles away it doesn't take long for war drone pilots to develop a sense of detachment. It's a stressful job that wears you down physically and mentally over time, which is why pilots like the new Ryan Decker are able to request and receive large blocks of vacation time.

Decker used his time to create a system that could fly multiple drones in tandem. He only acquired nine drones, but knew that nine, properly equipped and deployed, would allow him to kill 5,000 civilians in less than six minutes.

PART FOUR:
The Swarm

Chapter 1

Donovan Creed.

CALLIE'S STILL NOT talking to me, but she's done something I haven't been able to do. She's cracked the case wide open.

My first call is to Sherm Phillips. I tell him to contact the U.S. Marshals Service and get us the most recent photo of Austin Rennick.

My second call is to my drone expert, Charlie Whiteside, of Colby, California. Charlie was one of the original Edwards Air Force war drone pilots, and one of the early victims of psychological burnout. After leaving the military, Charlie wound up flying UAV's for the California Coastline Weather Service. Years ago, when crime boss Joe DeMeo declared war on my family. I paid Charlie to hijack a drone and perform a detailed reconnaissance on DeMeo's estate. Thanks to Charlie, who stands only 32 inches tall, I was able to deploy my army of little people to the best possible advantage. We overwhelmed Joe, I dodged a lethal threat, and Charlie went back to videoing cloud formations.

After making some small talk I ask if he knows the name Ryan Decker.

Like everyone else in America, he does.

I tell Charlie that Decker has a fleet of nine armed drones. We don't know where they are, or what he plans to attack with them, but we know his intentions are bad, and the attack is imminent.

"I've heard of swarm piloting as a theory," Charlie says, "but I didn't know anyone was actually doing it yet."

"Apparently Decker figured it out. So how do I go about finding him?"

"Nothing could be easier. You're looking for a guy with current or previous war drone experience. This is a club with less than 1,500 members. You know he's in the U.S., so that knocks the number in half. Send his photo to the CIA, Army, Navy, and Air Force. They should be able to ID the guy within minutes. They'll tell you where he served and when he left. And if he's still active, you're ahead of the game."

"We should have the photos within the hour. But suppose he launches the drones before I can pinpoint his location. How can we shoot them down?"

"It's not an issue."

"Why not?"

"He doesn't have military-grade drones."

"Assume he does."

"He doesn't."

"Fine. But pretend he does. It'll help me understand how the damn things work."

"If he had military-grade war drones we could jam the signal, and there's a good chance the drones would stop in midflight and fall safely to the ground. Or they could fall to the ground and blow up."

"I hope you know that's not a viable risk for us to take."

"I'm just thinking out loud here, for the sake of argument."

"What was the other option?"

"If we could intercept the signal, we could possibly reset the GPS parameters."

"Could you, personally, land the drones safely?"

"Individual drones? Certainly. A swarm? Probably not. Can I tell you why none of this matters?"

"Go ahead."

"Decker doesn't have military-grade drones."

"Convince me."

"The entry-level price for military-grade armed drones is $22 million. And they're huge, with wingspans of 45 to 110 feet! No way Decker has nine of them, or even one. He couldn't keep it a secret."

"What if he has access to them? What if they're in Mexico or South America, and he's working with a terrorist group? Couldn't he launch them from there? From what I understand they can be launched from 7,000 miles away."

"And further. But you're missing the point. He wouldn't try to attack Americans using military-grade drones."

"Why not?"

"These types of drones require sophisticated space-based guidance systems that are monitored and controlled by the military. They're totally reliant on GPS-based navigation, so the military would instantly know about an unauthorized launch."

"Pretend I'm twelve years old and have no idea what you're talking about."

"If you're in your living room watching TV and I break into your house and start frying bacon in your kitchen, how long would it take you to figure it out?"

"Seconds."

"There you go."

"So Decker doesn't have military-grade drones."

"That's correct."

"Then why didn't you say so in the first place?"

"Funny."

"Still, I've been told he has nine armed drones. What type could they be?"

"Line-of-sight."

"What's that mean?"

"If he truly has nine drones, they're small and primitive. So primitive he has to be able to see what he's attacking. For example, he could line them up on a runway, drive a short distance toward the target, and stand on top of a building. Then he could launch them, have them fly past him, and he could steer them toward the target. But he would have to be able to see the target."

"So he has to be within a mile or two of the target."

"If he's an urban terrorist, I assume it's an urban target. So we're talking a mile or two, max, and we're talking daytime."

"What about night vision?"

"Too restrictive. Too many variables."

"If he launches, how do we stop him?"

"We don't. If he launches, and his system works, his mission will be successful."

"How big a payload could these tiny drones carry?"

"Think of it as if he had a hand grenade under each wing. Eighteen in all."

"Dropped where? The White House?"

"No. We're talking about an outdoor gathering of people, because the payload's too small to blast through fortified structures and cause widespread casualties."

"So theme parks, political rallies, Fourth of July celebrations?"

"Exactly. And don't forget the Kentucky Derby, Indianapolis 500, outdoor football games...any event that would draw a large outdoor crowd."

"I'll get my geeks on it. As far as where he might be keeping the drones, what am I looking for?"

"A large tract of isolated real estate near an urban area, either purchased or leased. Because if this guy's been testing nine drones, he needs space to practice. And a runway."

"How long a runway? How wide?"

"Good question. I don't know."

"Best guess."

"Depends on if the drones are linked width-wise or length-wise. My guess is width-wise, but that would require an area the size of a parking lot. Unless he can link them once they're in the air, which would be really sophisticated. If that's the case, he could probably make due with a 300-foot driveway."

I thank Charlie for his help and ask him to be available 24/7 till this is over. He's glad to oblige. I would be, too, if I spent my days monitoring cloud formations.

My third call is to the geeks. I tell them what to do when Decker's photo comes through. I also tell them to look up every outdoor event in America that's expected to draw at least 100,000 people this year.

My fourth call is to Jill DiPiese, to find out what the hell's going on. But Jill's phone no longer works, and her safe haven has been abandoned. She's either with Decker, or she's turned into a Decker sympathizer. Either way, she's number two on my hit list. People died because she chose to protect this mass murderer. My daughter's in serious condition—might even have brain damage—partly because Jill chose to give us a phony description of him.

My fifth call is to Milo Fister. I agree to take the hit and tell him we can work out the details after I kill Maybe Taylor. I assure him the dollar cost will be a fraction of what Maybe charged, and they won't even have to pay her now.

He's happy.

Just as I start wondering how Callie's doing, she calls.

"Have you blinked yet?" I ask.

"Yes. You win. Congratulations."

"I thought you'd hold out longer."

"I would have, if Decker's goons hadn't attacked us in the hotel room."

"*What?*"

Chapter 2

"DECKER'S MEN ATTACKED you?"

"Yup. Moments ago."

"Shit! Are you okay?"

"I am. But Jack isn't."

"What happened?"

"After you hung up I kept questioning Jack and got some additional information you'll want. But all of a sudden I felt a change in the air. I knew something was wrong."

"Instinct."

"Yeah. It just felt wrong. I kicked down the door to the adjoining room. Decker's men were obviously in the hall, or had just arrived. When they heard the noise, they started shooting. Sprayed the room with gunfire."

"They didn't try to enter?"

"No. They fired about 40 shots and hauled ass. They were totally unprofessional. All their shots went high except the trailers. Those are the ones that got Jack."

"He's dead?"

"Probably. I couldn't afford to wait around, so I taped his leg to stop the bleeding. It's bad. If he lives he'll lose the leg."

"My bet? You saved his life. No one uses tape like you."

"Thanks. I hope so."

My cell phone vibrates with a new text message. I say, "You're sure you're okay?"

"I'm fine. I was in the adjoining room."

"Thank God. By the way, I just got a text from Decker."

"What did it say?"

"I haven't checked yet."

"Go ahead," she says. "I'll wait."

"Are you sure?"

"Yes. I have something to say, but it can wait."

"Tell me now."

"You should check the message. Decker's planning a major attack. It could be important."

"It *could* be important. But whatever you've got to say *is* important. Decker's message can wait."

"Okay, I'll make it quick. I'm breaking up with you."

A cold chill runs through my veins. All I can think to say is, "Why?"

"I've got jealousy issues. You're probably thinking, 'Really?' But yeah, it's a sickness, and it's only going to get worse."

"Let's work on it. Together."

"No. It's a sickness. It's preventing me from doing my job properly."

"You cracked the whole case just now."

"And nearly got killed in the process."

"Your instincts were dead on."

"Quick question. What happened in the limo between you and Jill?"

I frown. Jack said something. I fight the urge to sluff it off. "The truth is she came onto me. She took her clothes off, fondled herself, and I didn't stop her."

"I believe you. But we had a discussion about this very subject. Do you remember?"

"Yes. And when I heard your view on it I told you the truth. It will never happen."

"But it did."

"Yes. Prior to our discussion."

"An honest man would have confessed."

"An honest man might be prepared to lose you. I wasn't. And I'm still not."

"I'm not pointing fingers, I just wanted to hear you say it. But I'm no better, Donovan. In fact, I'm ten times worse."

"What do you mean?"

"Did Decker attach a video to his text?"

"Yes."

"When you view it, you'll never want to see me again. You'll probably try to kill me."

"How bad could it be?"

"The worst you can think of, times ten."

"Callie, I don't care if you *slept* with the man. It won't change things between us. Not if you want us to work out."

"Our relationship was doomed from the start. It's all passion and no trust. And...can I be honest?"

"Of course."

"The sex wasn't all that great."

I chuckle despite the fact my heart is breaking.

"What's so funny?" she asks.

"Give me another chance. I'll work on the sex part."

"You won't want to after watching Decker's video. You'll see I'm right. And Donovan?"

"Yeah?"

"Feel free to blink."

"I did. As soon as you told me about the attack."

"I lied."

"About what?"

"Blinking during the attack. I never did. I won."

I chuckle again. "I'm going to miss you like crazy."

"Me too. And if you decide to kill me after watching the tape, please give me the courtesy of warning me first."

"There's nothing you could ever do that would make me want to kill you."

"We'll see."

"You want to hold on while I watch it?"

"Sure, why not?"

I click on the message from Decker. It says: *I think you'll find this interesting. I certainly did.*

I click on the video....and can't believe what I'm seeing.

I'm witnessing a crime.

I'm watching Kathleen being brutally murdered by Callie.

Chapter 3

AS THE VIDEO rolls, I feel something I haven't felt in years: a stabbing pain in my chest. I know it's stress. I close my eyes, try to breathe deeply, try to make the pain subside. I open my eyes, stand, walk around the room, take deep breaths.

She killed Kathleen.

And not in a quick, painless manner.

Callie's right. I'll never get the image out of my mind. One moment she's cradling Kathleen's head in her hands, the next, she's smashing it against the concrete floor, again and again. It's not a fake. Callie's admitted it, in her own way.

And worse....

She knew Decker had the video.

Which means he was blackmailing her.

That's who she was texting when we left the crime scene in Jackson, Mississippi.

As bad as killing Kathleen is—and it's really bad, because by doing so she turned Addie into an orphan again—she withheld information that could have saved people's lives. Could've kept Kimberly from getting hurt.

I shake those assumptions out of my head. There has to be another explanation. Callie wouldn't betray her country to keep me from learning about Kathleen. She didn't know Decker was planning to bomb those houses. She didn't know Kimberly was there. I need to ask her how much she knew, and when she knew it.

And I would, if I could speak.

But right now?

My God! The way she smashed Kathleen's skull was....inhuman.

I walk around the room a couple more times, till the pain subsides. Then I click the phone to bring Callie back.

We listen to each other breathe a minute. Finally she says, "Say something."

"Decker blackmailed you."

"Yes."

"You covered for him?"

"A little."

"Tell me."

"He placed cameras throughout Kathleen's house and garage. I'm not sure what their relationship was, but he was in the house when I killed her. If only I'd known. He obviously knew Kathleen, and had some sort of plan for her. I'm not blaming them for what I did. I'm a psychopath."

"How much did you know about Decker?"

"I promised I wouldn't personally help you find or kill him. I agreed to recommend that you pay the ransom."

"What else?"

"That's it."

"Did you know in advance about the bombings?"

"No."

"But he texted you about Kimberly."

"When he learned she was in the hospital he planned to kill her. I made a deal with him. He agreed not to kill her if I killed Jack."

"But that was a setup."

"I think so."

"Which means Kimberly's at risk."

"Not if you're guarding her."

"The police have two men at the door. There are detectives and FBI present, as well."

"Why?"

"One of the homeowners hired her to kill his wife and her lover. And she did. But like Decker said, she was in the wrong place at the wrong time."

"You don't think there was a connection? That Decker planned the bombing around Kimberly?"

"No. He also bombed Jackson, Mississippi. The locations were carefully selected. There's no way he could have known that far in advance where Kimberly would fulfill the hit. Now answer the important question."

"What's that?"

"Why'd you kill Kathleen?"

Chapter 4

CALLIE SIGHS. "I killed her because I'm flawed. I love you so much I get worked up and freak out when the first thing goes wrong. I went to see her because I was angry she met you for dinner. I didn't like her attitude, or the way she treated you. I hated her and couldn't understand why you ever loved her. You nearly married her a few years ago, and I wanted to find out why."

I suddenly remember how Callie made love to me this last time. "You went there to find out about her sexual technique."

"If you figured that out, you're as bad as I am. No offense."

"Things got out of hand and you killed her."

"No. I made her call you. I listened in."

"I remember. It made no sense, her calling like that. We made it clear at dinner the night before."

"I know. But I warned her to never call you again. And told her if she did, I'd kill her."

"And she *did* call. While I was on the phone with you."

"Yes. And you told me she had something important to tell you."

"You thought she was going to tell me about your threats. So you went back to her house and killed her. Decker saw the video and called you to blackmail you."

"Yes. And shortly after that I found pictures of you, naked, in Kathleen's bed."

"After you killed her?"

"Yes."

"That was before you and I made a commitment to each other."

"By two days."

"I'm sorry about that. And I should also mention I had a one-night stand that same night with the woman who hired Kimberly to kill her husband."

"*What?*"

"I know. It's a crazy coincidence. If you read this in a novel, you'd call bullshit on the author."

"I was more surprised you fucked two women in the same day. And that's a perfect example of why we could never work. We're both cold-blooded killers, but you're a hound dog. What happened to Kathleen is the same thing that happened to Eva. And might happen to you."

"Again, you and I weren't together when I saw Kathleen and Faith."

"See how casually you put that? You said you *saw* them. That eats me alive, Donovan."

"I know. And I'm sorry. And sorry about Jill."

"Thanks for saying so. The bottom line is you're you and I'm me. I wish it didn't bother me that you have a tendency to stray. But I've known you too long to trust you for any period of time."

"I understand." I pause a moment, then say, "Can I ask you three questions?"

"Please."

"One: do you want to keep working with me?"

"I'd love to. If you can forgive me for the Kathleen thing."

I consider pointing out how casually she said *that*, but instead, I say, "I'm willing to try. Regardless of our relationship, the country needs you. Your personal demons are a constant struggle, but they're the reason you're so good at your job."

"Thank you. I think. What's your second question?"

"You agreed to kill Jack. Why didn't you?"

"Decker told me to kill Jack without questioning him. So I knew Jack had some valuable information that could help us catch Decker."

"Why did you break your promise to Decker?"

"Is that your third question?"

"No. It's a bonus question."

"He committed an act of terrorism against our country. And no, I didn't consider writing graffiti on people's asses to be terrorism. But when you bomb their homes, all bets are off."

"Even though you knew he'd send me the tape of Kathleen."

"Whatever happened to us, or whatever you decided to do to me, was less important than stopping Decker."

"I believe you."

"Thank you. What's your third question?"

"Did you even pause to consider the effect it would have on Addie to murder her mother?"

"Barely."

I remove the phone from my ear and stare at it a moment, in disbelief. Then I return it as she adds, "Don't even think about playing the orphan card with me! You've turned *hundreds* of kids into orphans. It's supposed to suddenly be different because you used to date Kathleen? That's bullshit! You said you're over her. Either you are or you aren't. I threatened her, she ignored me, I killed her. It's what we do, Donovan. It's what we've always done. It's who we are. We kill people, and we create orphans."

I take it all in and realize she's right. I hate the fact she killed Kathleen. But it would be the height of hypocrisy to point a finger at her when I've done much worse.

I finally say, "I have another question."

"You're starting to get on my nerves," she says.

I'd smile, but the subject's too serious. I ask, "Are you sorry you killed Kathleen?"

"No," she says, without a moment's hesitation.

We listen to each other breathe a few more minutes while I try to comprehend how her mind works, and how she could possibly function in society.

And I'm positive she's thinking the same thing about me.

Finally, I say, "Is there anything else I should know?"

"Am I still on your payroll?"

"Yes."

"Are you going to try to kill me?"

"No. You have my word."

She pauses a long time, then says, "No. I have nothing else to tell you...at this time."

I don't like the sound of that, but I let it go. For now. I say, "Do you want to try to make things work between us?"

"Are you kidding?"

"Yes."

"Good. Because like I said a minute ago—"

"The sex wasn't great?"

"For me, no. I'm sorry, I did try. How about you?"

I say, "You're the best I ever had."

"Really?"

"Really."

She says, "I thought I might be. Especially at the end."

"You were great."

"And you're a lying sack of shit. I was terrible, and we both know it."

"I've been with worse."

"No one would doubt that. Let's move on. If I'm still on your payroll, what do you want me to do next?"

"Can you get a nurse's uniform?"

"Sex is off the table, big guy. But I have a lead on Decker, if you're interested."

"What do you mean?"

"While I was taping his leg, Jack told me where to look for the drones."

"You took the time to let him write it out?"

"He was determined to help. There he was, on his back, taped to the chair, his leg practically cut in two, bleeding profusely, and he never let go of the ink pen."

"I'm impressed."

"I was, too."

"What did Jack have to say that was so important?"

Chapter 5

CALLIE'S GOOD NEWS—that Decker has a small piece of acreage in New Albany, Indiana—is shattered by the bad news I receive from the geeks.

It started off promising enough. Curly, Larry, and C.H. said the military made a positive ID on Decker. He's active duty, operating out of a command center in Indianapolis. His photo's being disseminated to law enforcement throughout the country as we speak. The fact that he's currently on vacation isn't the bad news.

The bad news is Curly gave me the earliest possible outdoor target. It's an event taking place today, right now, on the banks of the Ohio River, in the very city where I'm standing.

Louisville, Kentucky, just as Decker planned.

And Louisville's located directly across the river from New Albany.

My head's swimming. I have to act quickly. I call the geeks and tell them to search New Albany property records going back the past five years. I want every tract of land larger than two acres that's been sold or leased within five miles of Louisville's riverfront. I tell them to check under Decker, and his aliases, and Jack Tallow, and his aliases, and even toss in Jill and Bobby DiPiese for good measure.

Now what?

I'd like to call the Louisville Police Department and have them force an evacuation of the event. Problem is I have no legal authority to demand anything, since, in the eyes of law enforcement, my agency doesn't even exist. They probably wouldn't even put my call through to the chief of police.

I think about calling in a bomb threat, but if Decker's just toying with me, and doesn't intend to attack today, there'll be hell to pay with Homeland Security.

I call Sherm Phillips and say, "I need you to issue an order to get choppers in the air above New Albany, Indiana. And to suspend the air show going on right now in Louisville."

"Why?"

"Ryan Decker might be launching a drone attack on the crowd today."

"How many people are we talking about?"

"Up to 800,000."

"*What?* For an *air* show?"

"The air show precedes Thunder Over Louisville, the world's largest fireworks display. It kicks off the Kentucky Derby festivities."

"How could this guy acquire a drone? How could he operate it?"

"He's got nine drones hooked up to a single control. He's planning to fly them line-of-sight, which means he's got to be within a few miles of downtown Louisville. Assuming he plans to attack."

"You need surveillance choppers?"

"Yes. We're looking for a small runway or parking lot within three miles of downtown Louisville, probably in New Albany. Decker will likely be standing on top of a building. If he is, he should be easy to find. If you can get a shooter on board to take him out, we might be able to wrap this up."

"I'll give the order, but if the attack is imminent, we may not get there in time. Do you have a contingency plan?"

"You could contact the news stations in and around Louisville. They already have choppers in the air to report on the crowds and air show. If one of these pilots, or one of the air show pilots, sees nine small drones flying toward the river, I hope you'll give the order for them to crash into the drones."

"They're armed?"

"Yes. It would be a suicide mission."

"Not many would do that."

"I bet you're wrong about that."

"I can't order civilians to commit suicide."

"Then get me a news chopper to take me to New Albany. If I can't find the drones before they launch, I'll have the pilot drop me into their path. I guarantee you I'll stop those things."

"Hopefully it won't come to that."

"I hope not. We know Decker either bought or leased some land in New Albany. My guys are searching property records. If we find it soon, I might be able to prevent the attack."

"I'll get you a chopper."

Chapter 6

Ryan Decker.

THUNDER OVER LOUISVILLE lures up to 800,000 spectators to the banks of the Ohio River. If Decker could fly his birds at night, he could kill 5,000 of them and wound many more. But he can't fly them at night.

Can't fly them anywhere, for that matter, since the damn things are broken.

They worked during the initial run, two months ago, for a very short flight. Think Wright brothers, at Kitty Hawk.

But in the second effort, for reasons Decker can't explain, four of the craft veered sharply into the others with disastrous results. The effort to rebuild and retest proved too substantial for Decker's time and financial resources, so he focused his attention on a two-stage bombing process that involves firing a thermobaric warhead into a mushroom cloud of conventional explosive laced with aluminum powder. The destruction of Jack's house in Willow Lake offered a glimpse into the destructive power Decker possesses.

He put the word out among jihadists, revolutionaries, and insurgents throughout the world that his drones were working perfectly, and he possessed the munitions and technical ability to deliver a lethal strike.

And the money poured in.

Decker figured Creed's people would eventually hear about it, and he'd be able to use the drone rumor as a diversion. When they didn't, he decided to put things in Callie's hands.

And she delivered.

Decker didn't want to rat Callie out by sending the video to Creed, but if he hadn't followed through on his threat, she'd be suspicious. And Decker needs them to be concerned about a drone strike.

He laughs, thinking about the dozen teenagers he hired to stand on top of buildings in downtown New Albany today. And how eight of his men are positioned on two speedboats in the Ohio River, anchored a scant 100 yards from the riverfront crowd that has gathered to watch tonight's fireworks program. They're just two boats among hundreds that'll stay all evening until the fireworks spectacular ends around 9:45.

At 9:15, when the fireworks begins, all eyes will be up, focused on the display.

What a perfect time for his men to break out their shoulder-fired rocket launchers and begin shooting randomly into the crowd! If five shells can bring down a multi-million dollar mansion, imagine what sixteen shells can do to a throng of wall-to-wall people who won't even hear the shots fired because of the fireworks!

Each man will fire two missiles before the speed boat pilots race upriver to the Westport landing, where four cars will be parked, with engines running, guarded by a fifth car. The boats will run right up onto the landing, and Decker's men will jump into the cars and drive away at normal speed and blend into the night.

Decker won't be there to witness the attack.

He's in Gamble County, Missouri, waiting to launch a rocket into the mushroom cloud that's about to appear above the Gamble County Art Show and Bean Festival.

Every year more than 40,000 visitors make the trek to the area of Gamble County where two old highways converge. Since the nearest hospital is 35 miles away, the festival area is virtually isolated from medical care.

This was no coincidence. Decker chose this particular venue because a big part of the human drama will be provided by the multitude of bloody victims who could have been saved had there been proper medical care. But county officials, using past festivals as their guide, decided two medical vans would be sufficient to care for those who might overeat, drink, or suffer dizzy spells from getting too much heat.

Decker searches the sky till he sees his pilot. He waits for the drop, then the explosion, then the mushroom cloud. He fires his missile into the cloud even as 40,000 dazzled visitors are oohing and awing at what they consider to be part of the festivities.

He'd love to witness the carnage first hand, but that would be stupid. And anyway, he can see it on TV from a safe place later tonight. He ditches the rocket launcher and begins the long drive to Salina, Kansas, where he'll meet Jill, who insisted on being there when he kills her husband, Bobby DiPiese.

Chapter 7

Donovan Creed.

I'VE NEVER BEEN to Thunder over Louisville, or I would've known about the hundreds of boats I now see beneath me on the river. I'm hovering above the downtown bridge that serves as the focal point of the fireworks display scheduled to take place hours from now.

Captain Chaz, my helicopter pilot, senses my concern.

"What's wrong?" he asks.

"Who searches those boats and the people on them?"

He looks down at them and says, "No one, far as I know. But I'm sure the Coast Guard keeps an eye out, in case someone's drinking, or tossing trash in the river."

"You've got hundreds of boats anchored between two riverbanks."

"So?"

"Each riverbank has hundreds of thousands of spectators."

"It's *always* been that way. What's your point?"

"The boats are within rifle range of both river banks."

He looks down again and says, "Holy shit!"

I try to call Sherm, but he doesn't answer, so I press a button on my cell phone and watch Chaz's eyes grow huge when I say, "Mr. President? Sorry to call, but I'm on a Sky News 80 helicopter, and I've identified a huge security risk."

"Does it involve our current concern?"

"Not directly."

"Then I'd say don't allow yourself to get distracted."

"I can't ignore it. There are hundreds of boats within rifle distance of both riverbanks. One boat crew with automatic weapons could bring down thousands of spectators."

He sighs. "I hate talking to you, Creed. Every time I do I lie awake at night, worried about how much damage you could do to our country if you ever flipped. What's your recommendation with regard to the boats?"

"Have the Coast Guard send them home."

He sighs again. "Telling those boaters to clear out would be like shutting down a UK-UL basketball game at halftime."

"I have no idea what you're trying to say."

"It would cause a riot."

"Mr. President, when having access to a boat is the only qualification required to anchor within shooting distance of a hundred thousand people, a riot is perfectly acceptable."

"What if I ask the Coast Guard to conduct a thorough search of the boats?"

"Poor substitute."

"Why?"

"There are hundreds of boats and only a few Coast Guard vessels. And more boats are heading toward the area by the minute. Dozens could slip in while the Guard is busy conducting searches."

"Can boats get to the area from both directions?"

"No sir. There are locks to the west."

"These are mostly small boats, correct?"

"Yes sir. But most are cabin cruisers."

"We'll place one Coast Guard vessel east of the crowd to cordon off the area. Meanwhile, the remaining vessels can conduct a boat-by-boat search. Would that satisfy you?"

"Yes. But make sure the Coast Guard flashes their lights and announces their intentions by radio and megaphones."

"Why?"

"Because if someone's got weapons on board, they'll try to escape."

"Good point. I'll get the message out immediately."

"Thanks."

"What about New Albany?"

"We're heading there now, to search rooftops and parking lots."

"You should have some company. Every news station within 100 miles has sent choppers. If Decker's on a rooftop, we should find him pretty quickly. By the way, you're on speaker phone. Sherm Phillips says if you need anything else, call him."

"Sherm, what's the ETA on the military choppers?"

"There is none. We re-routed them to Gamble County, Missouri."

"Why?"

"Decker, or one of his men, fired one of those two-step bombs over a festival crowd of 40,000 people. I'm extremely disappointed you didn't alert us. It was exactly what you were concerned about: an outdoor event that draws tens of thousands of people."

I'm stunned. He's right, it's my fault. I told my geeks to start with events that draw crowds in excess of 100,000 people. I planned to start there, and widen the parameters later.

I ask, "How bad is it in Missouri?"

"Really bad. But focus on New Albany in case Missouri was a diversion."

"We can't get any military support at all?"

"We've got the National Guard on standby. But we can't roll them in without a definitive reason."

"I've got a witness who says Decker plans to launch a drone attack. Isn't that a definitive reason?"

"Not without a date and location," Sherm says. "Give us a reason, I'll send in the Guard. Anything else?"

"Yeah. Why didn't you call to tell me Decker bombed a crowd in Missouri? Don't you think that information could be helpful to me?"

"I hold you personally responsible for failing to alert us about that festival. We've got a call list, Creed. And because you fucked up I moved you so far down the list your local ice cream truck driver will get the news before you."

"It's great to be appreciated."

"Fuck you!"

In the background the president says, "Thanks for your service!"

Chapter 8

THE FIRST GUY I see standing on a roof in New Albany looks all wrong, even from this distance. So does the second guy. And the third.

"What are the chances this many men would be standing on rooftops in New Albany?" I ask.

"Normally I'd say zero," Chaz says, "But maybe they're waiting for the air show to resume."

"By themselves? No wife, kids, or friends? I doubt it."

It's clear Decker set us up.

As we circle the city, checking out the guys on the roofs, Geek squad Larry calls to ask if I heard about Gamble County, Missouri, and to apologize for not including that in their report.

"Not your fault, Larry. I set the parameters. Any word on the casualties?"

"No hard numbers, but it's really bad. Hundreds, they think. Maybe more."

He then gives me the coordinates of the small farm just outside New Albany that was leased a year ago to a Mr. A. Rennick, and I pass them along to Chaz.

"We would've caught it sooner," Larry says, "but we focused on New Albany first, and then started moving outward."

"You did the right thing."

"We do have some good news," he says.

"I could use some."

"The government declared the Louisville bombing a terrorist attack."

"Why's that good news?"

"It means our legal team was able to classify Jane Doe as a suspected terrorist. They're releasing her to our care. She'll be here, at Sensory Medical, in a few hours. These lawyers must be great. There were no objections."

"Not even the FBI?"

"No sir. They've already left the hospital. Kimberly's medevac has been green-lighted all the way."

"No one knows who she is?"

"Just the two who hired her."

"I'll deal with them soon enough."

"Should we keep searching for farms in the area?"

"Yes. There could be more than one."

"The one I gave you has two outbuildings. Maybe you'll find the drones there."

"I hope so."

Within minutes Chaz sets us down on a level area of farmland and says, "I don't know what to do. Am I likely to get shot?"

"No. I doubt there's anyone or anything in these sheds. But if someone shows up, honk the horn."

"Horn? Helicopters don't have horns."

"No shit?"

"Why would we need a horn?"

"To make other choppers get out of the way."

"But—"

"It was a joke, Chaz."

"Oh."

"Relax. I'll be right back."

I was wrong. There *is* something inside one of the sheds. I call Sherm.

"Tell me something good," he says.

"I found the drones."

"*What? No shit?*"

We located Decker's farm. He's got two storage sheds. One's empty, the other contains nine drones in various stages of disrepair."

"The lying bastard never had the technology."

"It appears that way. But you need to send some guardsmen to secure this equipment. Some of these drones look operable."

"In your opinion is the drone threat over?"

"Unless he's got more than nine. According to my expert on the subject, that's unlikely."

"It has to be your call, Creed."

"Sherm, you've become a politician."

"I can't be much help to you if I lose my job."

"And if I lose mine?"

"You don't have one, remember?"

"I do remember. It's a fact I'm reminded of every time I try to give an official order. Fine. I'm calling it."

"Say it for the record."

"The drone threat is over."

"Give me the location and I'll send some military to clean the site. Maybe we'll learn something after checking out his equipment."

"How soon can they get here?"

"Why? You got a date?"

"I need to get back to the hospital to interview one of the witnesses before she gets air lifted to Sensory Medical."

"Are you talking about Jane Doe?"

"Yes."

"You won't be interviewing her."

"Why Not?"

"She's brain dead."

I fall to the ground.

Literally.

The world is spinning all around me. I reach for my cell phone, but can't locate it. I notice Chaz, the pilot standing over me.

Is that a gun he's holding?

Chapter 9

IT'S NOT A gun. And Chaz is a news helicopter pilot, not a terrorist. And I'm a paranoid freak. Chaz helps me to a sitting position, hands me my cell phone. "Sherm?"

"What happened?"

"I dropped the phone. "What do you mean she's brain dead?"

"I'm surprised you don't know. Aren't you the one who wanted to medevac her to Sensory Medical?"

"Yes."

"Well, she'll be there in a few hours."

"There was only one Jane Doe, right?"

"Just the one. And I have no idea what you hope to gain from having her in your facility."

"Who pronounced her brain dead?"

"I don't know what you call them. Doctors, neurologists, whatever. For the FBI to be satisfied, it had to be thorough. You still want her at Sensory?"

"Yes."

I've got to get to the hospital to be with Kimberly. Got to figure out what's going on. Got to get her to Virginia, so we can restore her. But I have to wait for the National Guard to pick up the drones, because they represent a national security risk. If Callie were here, she could wait for them. But she's in New Orleans, in a nurse's uniform.

I should just leave and tell Sherm to have the ice cream guy take care of it, since he's so much more valuable than me.

I've got to do something, got to call the one person I know who can straighten this out. I press a key on my cell phone and Dr. Gideon Box answers while talking to someone else. I hear him say "Sorry, Mr. Chiles. I'm afraid our interview is concluded. I've got an emergency."

To me he says, "Hang on a sec, I'm on live TV. I need to get the microphones off."

It takes him 20 seconds to do that, then he says, "Sorry about that. What's up?"

"My daughter's been in an accident. She's been pronounced brain dead."

I hear Trudy in the background telling someone to take their hands off her. There are sounds of a scuffle, and a man shouting, "Ow! Shit! Get her *off* me!"

Dr. Box says, "Sorry, couldn't hear you. It's quite hectic here." He shouts, "*Trudy, let's go!*" Then gets back on the phone and says, "Who's been pronounced brain dead?"

"My daughter."

"Shit. I'm so sorry."

"What does that *mean?*"

"It means the doctors have done all they can to treat her. They're probably supporting the heart with oxygen and medication."

"So she's technically alive."

"No. They can keep her life functions going a few days, but brain death can't be reversed. It's final. Your daughter will never wake up, or recover."

"We've got the finest doctors in the world at Sensory Medical. That's where she's being taken. I want you there."

"I'm sorry for your loss, Donovan. But if she's brain dead, the only reason to keep her on life support is to harvest her organs. Is that your wish?"

"My wish is full and complete recovery."

"Personally, I'm quite fond of you. But you're a dangerous and highly unpredictable man. I'd rather not be in the same room with you when your daughter passes."

"Hours ago they said she'd be fine. Could they have misdiagnosed her?"

"At the time they said that, yes. But not now. Brain death diagnosis is virtually never wrong."

"*Virtually* never? So it *has* happened before?"

"I shouldn't have said that. I've given you hope. And there is none."

"There's always hope. And I expect you at Sensory Resources, prepped and ready, when she gets there."

"Prepped for what?"

"Whatever you guys do. You're going to find a way to restore my daughter's brain function."

"It's impossible."

"You think I'm *fucking* with you? If I have to come there and drag your ass to Sensory I can guarantee you'll regret it."

"I'm sorry, I didn't mean to upset you. I can be there in what, two hours? When is she expected to arrive?"

I take a deep breath. "I don't know. Three hours, give or take."

"I'll be there when she arrives, and I'll do all I can. But please don't kill me. I've finally gotten my life on track."

"You're completely without hope?"

"Yes. I'm sorry."

"I need you to believe."

"I'm sorry."

We're quiet a minute. He says, "Where is she now?"

"Mercy Hospital, Louisville, Kentucky."

"Can I ask why you don't want me to go there?"

"No one can know who she is. They can't know we're related."

"Why?"

"Don't focus on that part. Just tell me how they can know for sure she's brain dead. Doctors are human, they make mistakes. Kimberly was practically conscious a few hours ago."

"A number of criteria have to be met before the pronouncement of brain death can be made. She'd have to be in a permanent coma. They'd require proof all brainstem reflexes have ceased, and proof her breathing has permanently stopped. They would have ruled out other conditions, like extremely low body temperature, or drug or alcohol use."

"When she gets to Virginia, what will you do?"

"Your doctors are more qualified for this than me, but if you wish I'll instruct them to confirm the diagnosis with a lab test. But please don't get your hopes up."

"If you're convinced she's brain dead, what happens next?"

"You need to know it's highly unlikely her body will be functioning upon landing."

"What are the chances?"

"Less than five percent."

"I'll take it. I want her at my facility, where I can give her the best care in the world. And grieve, if we come up short."

"When she gets here, if she's alive, we'll perform the final test. If they say she's brain dead you may still be able to harvest her organs. If not, we'd give you time to say goodbye before shutting down the ventilator and other support machines."

"Do your best."

"Count on it."

One Year Later...

Chapter 1

Donovan Creed.

YOU'RE NOT GOING to believe this, but I built a house.

I'm serious.

I know it's the last thing you'd expect from me.

It's secluded as hell, more like a fortress, and has all sorts of nooks and crannies and secret rooms and escape tunnels and so forth.

It's not a huge house, but when you add up all the features, it's the most expensive private residence ever built.

You probably realize I couldn't have built it in the space of a year.

You're right.

I've been working on my dream house for years. I started construction after stealing billions from Sam Case. I originally planned to live here with Sam's wife, Rachel, but

323

at this point that's about as likely as Callie falling in love with Jake from State Farm.

Don't get me wrong, I'm not a complete homebody. I still break into people's houses, still occupy their attics. In fact, my home-away-from-home attics have grown to more than 20 cities in thirteen states.

But I only use them when fulfilling hits for the mob.

I quit my job with Sensory Resources, and yes, I miss working with the geeks more than you could imagine. But we stay in touch.

I also quit killing people, but as you can imagine, that didn't last. For years I convinced myself I was killing people who deserved it, and felt I was filling a hole in the justice system, making the world a better, safer place, and so forth, and maybe all those things are true. But the bottom line is I'm just like Callie.

We killed people because we're killers.

Are we the best in the world?

I honestly don't know. But we're the best we've met so far.

Callie and I are still working together, still killing people, but our romantic relationship ended the day I learned she killed Kathleen. Breaking up was definitely the right thing to do. As killers, we enhance each other's skills, but as a couple, we're poisonous. We bring out the worst in each other. I won't go into further detail. You get the point.

I *will* tell you what happened with Decker, though, because it's un-fucking-believable.

Chapter 2

DECKER'S ATTACK ON the Gamble County Art Fair wound up killing 4,615 people. It's the single worst terrorist act ever perpetrated on the American people.

And he nearly committed a worse one.

Thank God the Coast Guard began searching the boats on the Ohio River last year during Thunder over Louisville, because minutes after the search began, two speedboats tried to escape. They were confronted by the Coast Guard vessel the president positioned east of the festivities. A shootout ensued, and a number of liquored up Kentucky heroes saved the day.

Scores of boaters were already thoroughly pissed, having been denied the opportunity to travel downtown to watch the fireworks. When they saw two speedboats exchanging fire with the Coast Guard, they rightly assumed these speed-boats were the cause of all their problems. What they lacked in firearms, they made up for with courage. While the speedboat drivers attempted to evade the Coast Guard, a dozen motorboats rammed into them at full speed, knocking the shooters unconscious or overboard. The angry rednecks boarded the speedboats like ants on a Ding Dong and beat Decker's men half to death.

By the time the Coast Guard managed to calm everyone down and remove the randy rednecks from the speedboats, they discovered eight rocket launchers and sixteen missiles hidden in the holds. A short interrogation confirmed these were the same men that bombed the local neighborhood. Had 16 missiles been launched during the fireworks celebration, as planned, government experts estimate the body count could have exceeded 10,000.

Score one for the good guys.

In return for a reduced sentence, the eight members of Decker's bomb squad flipped on the rest of the bunch, and details began to emerge about the makeup of Decker's organization. As it turns out, Decker hired nearly 200 college-aged men and women to prank park guests and police at Central Park and Jackson Square. They did it for the fun, the fame, and a thousand bucks. I've already done the math for you: It cost Decker roughly $200,000 to write BWC on approximately 70 asses. That's nearly $3,000 per ass.

The cops arrested dozens of the kids, charged them with criminal mischief, sentenced them to probation and community service.

At least 90% of Decker's gang were arrested, including all the bombers. The Louisville group got life without the possibility of parole, and the Jackson bombers were sent to death row.

Both groups are appealing, and it'll take years before it's all sorted out. I'm not worried about justice being done. If the courts set them free, Callie and I will hunt them down. We've got names, photos, and addresses of all their family members.

Decker's the reason I retired.

Because—you may not believe this—the government caved in and paid him. Not the billion he asked for, but $100 million. Sherm Phillips was actually proud he settled with Decker for "ten cents on the dollar." With his entire gang off the payroll, Decker must have also been pleased with the number.

I'm livid about it.

Despite the fact his drones were damaged beyond his ability to repair them, despite the fact his swarm idea didn't work, despite the fact all his lieutenants were captured—the government felt it necessary to pay Decker to stop his attacks.

And they paid him with your tax dollars.

They fucking *paid* him!

It gets worse.

They also hired him as an anti-terrorist consultant!

This information is highly classified, and it goes without saying you're not supposed to know, so don't rat me out. I just felt you deserved to know what really goes on behind the closed doors in Washington.

I know what you're thinking: Decker died in a firefight with the FBI. You know this because you saw the footage on the evening news a thousand times and read the story in every newspaper and magazine and every social media platform on earth.

But it isn't true.

They faked his death, gave him a new face and identity, and now he's the safest man on the planet, because they think he's too valuable to kill.

Of course, when I heard all this I hit the ceiling. The CIA was so concerned about my reaction they lobbied the president to let them hunt me down and kill me. But no one on earth fears me like our president, so he gave me the same deal: $100 million dollars and a consulting contract to tell them all the different ways I could orchestrate successful terrorist attacks on the nation. Every month I send them a scenario that scares the shit out of them, and I suppose Decker does the same.

I know what you're thinking: I'm no better than Decker, profiting from this situation at your expense. But I didn't ask for the money, didn't offer my services as a consultant, never threatened the country, never attacked it, and never would. But taking the contract and the money prevents the CIA from killing me, same as I'm prevented from killing Decker. It may not be right, but it's how the world works.

Am I happy?

I do my best.

I'm not in a relationship, but I'm dating someone.

It's more of a sexual relationship. You're shocked, right?

I'll tell you about it after dinner.

But first you'll want to hear about Jack and Jill.

Chapter 3

JILL ALWAYS HAD a soft spot for Jack, and when she heard he'd lost his leg in a gun fight she insisted on visiting him in the hospital to check on him. Jill didn't know what Callie looked like, so she had no reason to suspect Callie was posing as one of Jack's nurses, or that she had bugged Jack's room and was listening to Jill's conversation.

Jill told Jack she was leaving New Orleans in a couple of hours to be with Decker. After wishing Jack a speedy recovery and saying goodbye, she took a cab to the airport and boarded a private plane. A quick flash of credentials gave Callie the plane's itinerary. She called to tell me Jill was flying to Salina, Kansas, to meet Decker. I took the call while standing at Kimberly's bedside at Sensory Medical, and forwarded the information to Sherm Phillips. Then I asked Callie to join me at Sensory. I wanted my best friend to be there when I said goodbye to my daughter.

Sherm contacted the FBI, and they arrived quickly enough to set up positions around the private airfield where Jill's plane was landing. Unfortunately, Decker must've sniffed them out, because he never showed. While waiting for Jill's plane to land, FBI agents discovered Bobby DiPiese's body in one of the hangars. When Jill's plane touched down, they arrested her. She's currently awaiting trial for aiding and abetting a known terrorist, providing false evidence to the police, conspiracy to commit murder, and assorted other charges.

She's expected to get life, but I guarantee she won't serve more than a month, because Decker's been pressing the government to release her. He worked a deal based on exposing some of the international terrorists he knows, and the government's just waiting for her trial to end. They'll put her in prison, fake her death, give her a new identity, new face, and she and Decker will live happily ever after.

Onward.

What else do you want to hear about?

I know.

Milo and Faith.

Good story. What happened was—

Wait. I just noticed the time. I've got a dinner guest.

A young lady.

Same one I meet every Thursday for dinner.

Let me enjoy this dinner date first, then I'll tell you all about Milo, and Faith, and about the sexual relationship I've been experiencing.

Chapter 4

THE DOOR OPENS. We hug, and I hold her a few extra seconds.

We walk to the den, I pour her a drink. She says, "How have you been, Daddy?"

I smile.

"Good. How's work?"

"Boring as hell."

I laugh. "You say that every week."

She shows me a pouty expression. "It's not fair. You and Callie go on missions all the time. You said it yourself, I'm one of the best you ever worked with."

I say what I always say: "We've been through this before. You beat the odds. You're one of only three people in the history of modern medicine who came back after being pronounced brain dead. I can't bear to lose you again."

"But I need a *life!*"

"That's exactly right. And you've got one. And when you meet the right guy...."

She rolls her eyes. "Daddy?"

I look at her.

"You know I love you," she says.

"But?"

"There's something we need to talk about."

I frown. "I know what you're going to say."

"You're sure about that?"

"Positive. But do me a favor and wait till after dinner, okay?"

She sighs. "Fine. But we're having this discussion."

"Okay."

"Tonight."

"We will. I promise."

Chapter 5

I HAVE TWO sets of cooks and housekeepers, but they don't live in the main house.

They work alternating weeks and while working, they live in subterranean wings of my house. While I'm a great boss, I require my employees to adhere to a strict set of rules. They're forbidden to speak about me, or the house, or any person who visits me, or anything that takes place inside the home, or on the grounds. During the weeks they're here, they're forbidden to leave their rooms for any reason unless I summon them.

Any reason.

If you come to visit me you'll not see any servants milling around the house, or listening outside the door like they do on *Downton Abbey*. My employees have a chip imbedded in their necks that burns like hell if they're not where they're supposed to be. It's easy to tell if someone isn't following the rules. They'll be grabbing their necks, shrieking in pain. My employees put up with these inconveniences because they each earn a quarter-million dollars a year and get every other week off.

And because I treat them with complete respect.

Apart from the neck thing, and a few strict rules.

Tonight my evening crew serves us a fine dinner, and Kimberly's cheeks have grown rosy from the wine. She's having a good time despite the fact her topic hasn't been discussed.

"Recognize the dish?" I say.

She stares at her food a minute. "It looks beautiful," she says, "and smells heavenly."

"It's the recipe you had in your pocket the night of the accident."

She looks at her pasta and smiles. "Thank you, Daddy."

"Enjoy."

When the conversation lags a bit, I ask, "How's your mom?"

"Have you talked to her?"

I laugh. "Are you kidding?"

She grins. "Mom's got a boyfriend."

"Omigod!"

"You're too old to say Omigod!"

"I was imitating you."

"Then say it right. *Omigod!*"

"*Omigod!*"

She laughs. "Not even close."

I try it a couple more times.

"Stop!" she says. "You're embarrassing me in front of the help."

"The help?"

She laughs. "Sorry. You know what I mean."

After dessert I dismiss the staff and Kimberly and I go back to the den. She says, "Can we talk now?"

"Can I pour you a brandy first?"

"No thanks. The two glasses of wine made me giggle like a thirteen-year-old all through dinner."

I look at her. "You were quite a handful at thirteen. I remember the time you—"

"Dad?"

"Yeah?"

"Stop avoiding the subject."

I take a moment, then sigh. "Okay. Go ahead. Say it."

"I can't do this anymore. I can't keep pretending I'm your daughter. You have to face the fact she's dead. It's not healthy to have me come here every week, pretending I'm Kimberly. I didn't sign on for this. Yes, you hired me to be her body double. But you also trained me to do bigger and better things. More important things."

"Kimberly, I—"

"*Layla*, Mr. Creed! My name is Layla Hart. Say it. *Please*."

"Is it a matter of money? I can pay you more."

She shakes her head. "Of course not. You're generous to a fault. You're paying me a king's ransom for a nice dinner every Thursday and a couple of phone calls during the week. I'd be crazy to give it up."

"Then why—"

She holds up her hand. "I'm worried about you, Mr. Creed. I'm worried about...your *sanity*."

"You're afraid I'll snap?"

She nods.

To be honest, I'm impressed with her integrity. Most people would gladly take the money and never say a word. They'd justify posing as Kimberly by saying they're helping me through a tough time. They'd call it therapy, and so would I.

We look at each other a moment.

I knew this was coming. It's been building up inside her for weeks.

I say, "Layla?"

Her face does a complete change. "Thank God!"

"You've been very therapeutic for me. Is that the right word?"

"I think so. At least, I know what you mean."

"What is it you'd like to do?"

"I'd like to work with you and Callie in some capacity other than the actual killing. I could work out travel arrangements, help you with research, provide support in a hundred different ways."

"But no dinners?"

"I'd be honored to have dinner with you anytime you wish. But not as Kimberly."

"Can you give me two weeks' notice? Just to get used to the idea?"

She thinks about it a minute, but says, "No. I'm sorry. It's just not healthy. For either of us."

"I understand."

"Mr. Creed, I'd be great at providing support for you and Callie. Or if there's something else I can do to help you—apart from the Kimberly thing."

"I'll think about it."

"Thank you."

I stand and offer to walk her to the door.

She stands, gives me a hug, and I use the opportunity to push a syringe in her butt and inject the sedative. Her body tightens instantly, then convulses, and I hold her till she loses consciousness. When she's completely out, I hoist her over my shoulder and carry her to her new chambers. I place her on the bed and remove her shoes to make her comfortable. She'll be difficult to deal with the first few days, but in the end she'll go back to playing the part of Kimberly.

Please don't worry about Layla.

I think the world of her, and won't keep her here a moment longer than absolutely necessary.

I'm just not sure how long that will be.

I *do* feel I'm making progress.

I'll keep you posted.

Chapter 6

YOU WANTED TO know about Milo and Faith.

When Kimberly arrived, and Dr. Box convinced me she was truly brain dead, I flew Milo and Faith to Sensory Resources. They didn't want to come, of course, but Callie was flying up from New Orleans anyway, so I asked her to stop in Louisville and talk them into making the trip. You know Callie. It didn't take her long to persuade them.

When they arrived at Sensory I placed Milo and Faith under house arrest while Callie and I spent some time hugging and commiserating, and standing beside Kimberly's bed. Although Kimberly never regained consciousness, her body managed to survive the trip, which, according to Dr. Box, was something of a miracle.

After Callie said her goodbyes to Kimberly, we summoned Milo and Faith, and I'll let you imagine the look on Faith's face when she saw me!

"That's right," I said. "I'm Movie Man, the guy you fucked in the men's room in Cincinnati a couple months ago. I'm also Maybe Taylor's father. Since you hired me to kill her, I'll let you watch while I pull the plug."

I did so, then asked Callie to take them to the car to wait for me.

After saying my final goodbyes to Kimberly, I drove Callie, Milo, and Faith to my new home.

I didn't show them around.

I told Callie to make herself at home in the den while I escorted Milo and Faith to my torture chamber.

I chained Milo to the wall. Then I handed Faith a knife and said she could either take her own life or his, but only one of them could leave the room alive. She tried to bribe me. Said she won the lottery and will soon collect more than a hundred million dollars. Said she'd pay me $10 million if I let her go. I told her if I ever get to the point where I need another ten million dollars I'll buy my own lottery ticket. She and Milo went through the whole spectrum of emotions you'd expect, but in the end, Faith carved him up pretty well, and I told her to drop the knife. She was reluctant to surrender her weapon, but I was in no mood to haggle.

We left Milo to bleed out, and I escorted Faith to her new chambers.

In case you're keeping score, I have six underground chambers on one end of my house for the household staff, and six additional chambers on the other end. There are also tunnels and passageways and various other subterranean rooms, and as you've heard, a torture chamber.

There's also a crematory for burning the bodies.

If Milo were alive he'd tell you all about it.

Faith's room, like Layla's, is equipped with a toilet, shower, bed, closet filled with clothes, TV, electronic tablets loaded with books, magazines, music, movies—everything a person could possibly require for an extended stay.

Apart from sharp objects, and the ability to communicate outside the house.

I waited a full six weeks before dating Faith...

Chapter 7

WHY SO LONG?

Lots of reasons. Shall I number them for you?

1. I wanted Faith to have time to adapt to her new surroundings.

2. I was still working for Sensory Resources, still trying to catch Decker.

3. I had to tell my ex-wife, Janet, what happened to her daughter.

4. I had to arrange Kimberly's funeral.

5. I had to get over losing Callie.

6. I had to approve Callie's detailed plan for Addie's future.

7. I had to talk Layla Hart into helping me cope with Kimberly's death. Although she'd been studying Kimberly's mannerisms for months, I spent countless hours coaching her in preparation for our dinners together. I gave her a wide range of scripts to learn, and encouraged her to improvise, so our Thursdays would always be unique and interesting.

8. And, of course, it took that long for the construction crew to turn one of my vacant subterranean chambers into an exact replica of the men's room of the hotel in Cincinnati where Faith and I had our first date.

Now, whenever it suits her—which is less often than you might think—I go to Faith's room, escort her to the men's room, bend her over the sink, and recreate that magical moment.

Am I happy?

I do my best.

Callie called a few minutes ago. Said she needs to tell me something about my former lover, Miranda.

"If you've killed her, you and I are done," I said.

"Relax. She's alive and well. My news is good...I think."

"Tell me."

"I'll tell you when I get there."

"Why not now?"

"I want to see the look on your face."

"The news is that good?"

"I honestly don't know how you'll take it. That's why I want to be there to see the look on your face."

"Whatever you've got to say, my face will show no emotion."

"We'll see about that," she said.

THE END

Personal Message from John Locke:

If you like my books, you'll LOVE my mailing list! By joining, you'll receive discounts of up to 67% on future eBooks. Plus, you'll be eligible for amazing contests, drawings, and you'll receive immediate notice when my newest books become available!

Let the fun begin here:
http://www.donovancreed.com/Contact.aspx

Or visit my website, http://www.DonovanCreed.com

John Locke

New York Times Best Selling Author
8th Member of the Kindle Million Sales Club
*(which includes James Patterson, Stieg Larsson, George R.R.
Martin and Lee Child, among others)*

John Locke had 4 of the top 10 eBooks on
Amazon/Kindle at the same time, including #1 and #2!

...Had 6 of the top 20, and 8 books in the top 43 at the same
time!

...Has written 19 books in three years in four separate
genres, all best-sellers!

...Has been published in numerous languages by many of the
world's most prestigious publishing houses!

Donovan Creed Series:

Lethal People

Lethal Experiment

Saving Rachel

Now & Then

Wish List

A Girl Like You

Vegas Moon

The Love You Crave

Maybe

Callie's Last Dance

Because We Can!

Emmett Love Series:

Follow the Stone

Don't Poke the Bear

Emmett & Gentry

Goodbye, Enorma

Dani Ripper Series:

Call Me

Promise You Won't Tell?

Dr. Gideon Box Series:

Bad Doctor

Box

Other:

Kill Jill

A Kiss for Luck

Non-Fiction:

How I Sold 1 Million eBooks in 5 Months!

Lightning Source UK Ltd.
Milton Keynes UK
UKOW06f2000260315

248599UK00005B/161/P